A Bleak New World

Andrews

Galford

Lucas

Maksym

Norris

Peery

Rick

Schwarzkopf

Townsend

Wollenfang

Raven International Publishing
Idaho Falls, ID

Introduction

Welcome to A Bleak New World. This book is packed with fantastic stories about society and our future. When we set out to put this project together we had no idea the positive response we'd receive. We were flooded with great submissions every day. It was difficult to pick the bests ones, but I think you'll agree that the authors in this anthology deliver an award winning reading experience.

I live for a world filled with peace, so why publish a book about dystopian societies? I have slogged through a lot of life, death of children, divorce, crises of faith, and then there was Iraq. What I did there and what I was willing to do there really made me look at myself in a negative light. When I got home I was drifting, had thoughts about killing myself or at least going back to the war. Some of my persona is a mask to hide that darkness, or at least keep it down. I want peace so badly in this life because I've seen the darkness. I feel that we need to confront those emotions and feelings and really look hard at ourselves. Through story we have that opportunity and that's why I'm excited to introduce this book to you.

I hope you enjoy A Bleak New World as much as I do.

Clark Chamberlain

Thank You

In today's book world, small presses like ours rely on fans like you sharing the love of our stories. If you like A Bleak New World, you can do this by telling your friends and family, and posting reviews to websites like Amazon and Goodreads.

We couldn't continue without your support and to say thank you we want to give you a free book. Just sign up for our email list and we will send you a digital copy of another great title from Raven International Publishing.

Sign up at www.RavenInternationalPublishing.com

Thanks so much, we can't do this without you!

For the dreamers who want a better world…

Touch Piece
Sealey Andrews

A great many years of my life were spent occupying, but not exactly *living on*, curio shelves. Rarely touched and never used. A novelty. For many boring decades I've also slept, ensconced in red velvet and darkness, tucked away from the world in a closet or attic. Safe keeping, I think they call it.

I've crossed continents. Sometimes given as a gift, sometimes a souvenir. A token from the past meant to conjure… I'm not even sure what, anymore. Long periods of time in a box will do that, disturb memories and understandings. Disturb the mind.

Before that, though, before my life as a token, I did have a purpose other than to simply be on show or kept as a protected thing from the past. I had a job. My life— my *body*—had meaning. I was designed to work, carved and sculpted in an artist's palm. There was a *need* to touch me.

And so there is again.

Today—now, in this time—it rains. A lot. Sheets of it

pelt the window every day. It has become the everyday.

When the water first started, the world called it a crisis. Rivers rose and spilled. Mountains slid into the oceans. The earth could not absorb anymore. The ground and the people became saturated. I was asleep in my red velvet bed through it all, though. A box in a box in a box in a box… But I have read the stories.

Brief reprieves allowed for some rebuilding, precious less-wet times that gave the people time to redefine how to live in this new, water-logged world. Technology was an immediate focus. Machine before man, of course. Man they are still working on.

It's raining again. Raining always. I draw in the condensation on the window. Win, the man whose desk I sit on now, will be in soon and I like to leave him pictures in the dew. Sometimes I draw him hearts. Other times I press my lips to the glass, planting teeny tiny kisses the size of snowflakes. And I always leave at least one long-forgotten, or shamefully never learned, Chinese characters that he should know, but doesn't. There is little preserved of the past now. Too much energy is focused on the future and *how* to live to stop the rain. There's not enough looking back and Win's heritage isn't the only one slowly being forgotten.

I suspect Win knows it's me leaving him fine point

pictures behind, as if drawn by a flower stem. Each morning when he arrives, he reads the characters and translates them with a few keystrokes on his keyboard. Then he runs the pad of his thumb over my cheek. Sometimes over my bare hip or a buttock, rubbing me like a touch piece—something carved for luck. But I am no Bixi, no stone tortoise. I am a girl. A woman. Alive.

At least when Win is away.

Outside the window, down, down below, people dart and dash in the rain. They shake themselves on door steps before seeking refuge in their shops and apartments. Street drains overflow with debris, rerouting water in channels and rivers through what used to be China Town.

From four stories up, I watch the umbrella tops go spinning by. They are the new means of expressing oneself, the only way to assert an identity—a personality—now that clothing is government regulated and issued. They are a mass of spinning pinwheels, their spokes a choreographed routine. They appear to propel everyone where they are going without ever catching a spoke. It's a practiced and perfect dance after all these years.

There are many bright and cheerful prints, comforting and uplifting against the grey misty backdrop. The women choose the best ones; I think. Elegant scrawling patterns, all that they are no longer allowed to wear on their bodies. Floral and paisley and toile. Even the occasional risqué—borderline illegal—lace. Or something that resembles it, at least. I'm not sure the world remembers what lace looks like anymore. Or brocade. Fabrics that you used to be able to run your hands over and *feel* their beauty, as much as see it, are now only two-dimensional constructions of what once was.

A french-fry container bumps and rebounds against the curb at the mouth of a street drain. I smile. It's a boat for me, I think, just my size. My imagination stretches the gum wrappers and bottle caps coming down the channel toward the drain. They are animals coming two by two like in a story I once heard a long time ago; the first time I came out of my box in this country. A story of a flood much like this one. A long, drawn-out cleansing of the earth. A ridding of temptation and sin.

One day, I believe, we will see and feel the sun again.

The familiar sound of Win's boots on the concrete steps directly below the window alert me that he is here. His umbrella is an ordinary flat black, his clothing standard issue and nondescript, but I know his trademark three *clunks* of each boot on that top step. The *kshhkshh* of his umbrella shaking off and the two taps he gives to it on the ground before entering the building.

Quick as a fox, I scamper barefoot—bare *everything*— across the desk, knocking a cup of styluses over in my dash to my balsa settee. I twist my waist-length hair into a hasty knot at the base of my neck and resume my daytime pose: on my side, legs crossed politely at the ankles, one hand behind my ear, the other unnaturally on my side. Why on earth a woman would ever choose to sit like this, I cannot fathom. Yet it is what I was fashioned to reflect.

The only reason I don't seize up from holding this torturous configuration all day is because Win has put me to use again. His need for me is what keeps me limber. I work for him, holding this position, serving his needs in the daytime. And in return, I am able to move at night. During the years when I was only looked on as decoration or nestled in my velvet lined box, I was forever stiff, my muscles taut and unyielding.

Win's office door opens then closes behind him. He shares this floor with two other practitioners. Two women. His office is the smallest. The walls are thin; the carpet is a red and scratchy indoor-outdoor, water-resistant variety. It runs up the walls about halfway to a thin rail of painted trim— black with peeling gold embellishment. It's something vine-like, a garish nod to the Orient that no one likely recognizes anymore.

Win coughs and grunts predictably; everyone has wet lungs these days. He hangs his jacket and umbrella over a drip pan behind his door. He runs his hands through damp hair as he takes a seat at his desk and rights the spilled cup of styluses with a pinched brow. When he sees my morning's gift on the window, he smiles, even if he doesn't know why.

Win has a patient. She doesn't come alone. She can't. She can't be in his presence alone. The law says so. It doesn't matter that he is a doctor. It doesn't matter that he has degrees hanging on the wall behind his desk, or that he is good and moral. Or that he is the most respectful and beautiful man I've ever known. And I have known more than just many.

There are only a few male physicians specializing in women's health now, distrusted and frightening to most. But my Win is stubborn. His almond-shaped eyes, set in creaseless lids, are bold and unafraid when he defends his career choice.

Patient and chaperone are dressed in grey gowns with matching grey fabric draped on their faces. Boring and drab and hot. Thick and musty with moisture. They are gowns that hide bruises. Not literal ones—black, blue, yellow—on the flesh, but sore places nonetheless. Places where the skin longs to be touched. To be worked.

Kneaded.

Needed.

After a few doctor-patient pleasantries, they get straight to work. Questions and answers only. Win is not allowed to touch her, of course. This is where I come in.

Win takes a stylus from the cup and hands it across the desk to his patient. He rotates me to face her. With the nib of the stylus she shows him what ails her by pressing on me in the places she hurts. It's a funny way, but a required way, at least for Win. Not for all doctors, though.

This is because, among the framed documents on Win's wall, there is one certification that is missing. The one that carries the most weight these days. One that would allow for him to do away with silly sticks and dolls. Win is not "touch certified." He technically knows what he is doing, as is proven by his degrees, and he is not forbidden to practice, but without the "touch" certification, it is an upward swim.

Win fears osteoporosis for his patient. Rickets, even. He gives her vouchers for the sun clubs where women can lay in beds of artificial sunlight and take in the vitamins their bodies are slowly getting used to not needing anymore. From his stocked apothecary cabinet, he pulls a few glass bottles for her. Supplements that will fill in the gaps until man (woman) evolves into not needing them anymore. She thanks him, and she and her escort leave. Sadly, she's his first and last patient of the day.

My box sits in the bottom drawer of Win's desk. Its presence there—so close, so accessible—is a constant reminder that my time is limited, that I am nothing more than a suture. Once the world knits itself back together again—gets itself right—I will go back in the box until someone decides again to pull me out, again as a useless but pretty thing to be put on a shelf once more.

Each generation will reap what the former generation has sown.

Four characters in the condensation await Win today. I don't intend for them to upset him. I only mean to be clever. But Win doesn't look at me after he translates them.

He is especially distressed these days, I've noticed. He doesn't look at my latest drawings— he doesn't touch me. Today he is buried deep in his head, alternating between reading an article in an online medical journal and glancing over his shoulder at the crookedly hung frames on his wall. He wears a look of longing and failure.

Win drags a stylus over his monitor. He taps on a photo and zooms. Suddenly, what he is agonizing over fills the screen in high resolution, and I know. *No!*

A document on your wall isn't the most important and telling thing you receive when becoming "touch certified." The most important thing you receive is something that you wear, something that publically authenticates you've been vetted. A collar.

The photo on the screen is of a masculine neck with

ropey veins and a bulging Adam's apple. Around it hangs an onyx ring of newly engineered polymer, strong as steel.

Win steeples his fingers at his chin. He sighs and stares at the screen. The phone rings. He answers pleasantly but turns curt midway through the conversation, ending with a soft apology. After Win hangs up, he taps at his monitor again, this time bringing up his patient contact book. He deletes an entry, and my heart sinks.

This. This is what is behind his mood. It's the third patient he's lost in as many days. If he, a man, is going to survive in this business, he needs that certification. He can no longer swim upstream; he is tired. I am realizing it just as he is. As good as he is at what he does, the truth is undeniable. Women want to be touched again.

Who can better understand this than me?

To get a collar, to become certified, you do not need money. It's not something that can be purchased like that. But that does not mean it doesn't come without a price. You give up your mind, or rather part of it. It's not just for males practicing medicine, like Win. There are many benefits to men having nothing to do with one's livelihood, things that make basic living just easier for men.

Collars make a man more approachable on the street. In fact, you become an ambassador of safety in this way. A man can entertain women in their homes who are not their wives, women without chaperones, if they so desire. Not that they would.

A collar marks a man as a candidate for marriage. Collared men can touch women however is needed, whenever it's needed, because there is no pleasure. There is no power. Collared men are trusted men. Surgically altered men.

Fashionably castrated men.

Win has come from his own doctor today. I know this because he has set a little glass bottle with his name on it next to his computer. And I am pretty sure I know what it's for.

Win left his computer up and running when he'd left his office the other day, something he doesn't do often. But on occasion, if I catch it before it goes to sleep and requires a password to reengage, I can get onto it. On these precious nights when he's been careless like this, I've read to my heart's content. Anything and everything; it's my only portal to the world outside and the way I first learned about the history of the water. A few days ago, that day he was so moody and distracted, he left it open to the article on collars. And I read.

Before a collar can be obtained, the article had said, and before certification is awarded, the patient must be administered a low-dose treatment of a hormone suppressing substance. It is given in the week preceding the surgery as a way of "stepping up" to what the collar will eventually take over doing—delivering what's needed through two metal receivers surgically implanted at the base of the neck, sending messages to disable the part of the mind that humanity has abused. If a patient doesn't properly "step up" with the drug, the collar installation will be fatal. They learned this the hard way during trials, I suppose.

When Win has gone for the night, I kick the bottle over. I scatter the pills across the desk in a childish rage. I know it is selfish of me to not want Win to be collared. I know how much easier his life will be because of it. And I know that he'll lose his practice if he doesn't bend to what the world calls for. But with certification there will be no need for *me* anymore. I won't have the luxury of simply waiting for the whole world to repair itself, however long that will take, before I will be put out of service. Win will put me out of service the moment the collar closes around his neck. And though it might not happen right away—he may keep me around for the memory or as a novelty for some time—eventually, I will be returned to my box.

On my hands and knees, I collect each pill and return them to the bottle. Every lift and drop into the container is done with a heavy heart. Every plastic-coated capsule I return to the bottle brings me closer and closer to losing Win. The last one I am reluctant to put back because of this. It's like putting it all back the way it was, pushing the bottle back into its position where he left it, is me colluding in his suppression.

I roll the capsule back and forth on the desk with my foot, stalling, feeling its contents shift inside its gelatin shell. Half pink, half yellow, such cheery colors for such a miserable fate. They should be black. Black like all the other government issued milieu of this world now. But no. They are pink and yell—I kneel down and examine the capsule. Funny, I hadn't noticed it at first, but it's the same color combination of one of the supplements Win prescribes to his patients. One he keeps on hand in his cabinet. That must be why he put this bottle by the computer, so as not to confuse them.

Win is on the last day of his "stepping up." I wonder if he's noticed. Has he felt any different this week? My guess is no. Pink and yellow. Yellow and pink. He drops the empty bottle in the recycle bin beside his desk.

I have left one last character in the condensation on the window. *Goodbye.* I doubt he understands the full weight of the farewell, though he thinks he does. He wipes it away with his sleeve and writes his own in its place. With bigger and broader strokes, it's clumsy and imperfect. Yet, I am still impressed. *New beginnings*, it reads. But not for Win, I'm afraid. I wonder if I should have drawn *I'm sorry* along with my goodbye.

The worst, most tragic event, I think, when the world went wet, was what happened to the cemeteries. Bodies were pried from eternal rest, caskets bobbed and sank. Lost. Too much attention was needed in other areas to stop the hemorrhaging and save the ones who still lived. The world moved on. Those who were lost, remain lost today. And no one is put to ground anymore.

Tombs and mausoleums are a necessity now. It's not what I want for my Win, but neither is what he had planned. And if I am destined to go into a box, so, too, shall he.

About the Author

Sealey Andrews is a Seattleite sushi lover, chronic organizer and list maker. She collects music boxes and miscellaneous odds and ends that are fun to touch. She enjoys the company of strangers more often than the company of friends and has a wicked addiction to Craigslist (but she's working on that).

Adores:

- words

- plants

- the female form

- all things body (and bawdy)

- chemoautotrophs

- Adam and Eve

- alliteration

- bullet points

Fears:

- butterflies (because nothing should move like that)

- large wild cats

- things with an unnatural gait (see butterflies)

- commas and semicolons

Sealey spends her nights traversing melatonin-fueled dreams and her days writing out the weird in her head. You can even read some of it online at Niteblade Fantasy and Horror Magazine, Liquid Imagination, SNM Horror Magazine, and Nanoism. Or, if you prefer the paper page, in the anthologies Sinisterotica and Uncle John's Bathroom Reader Presents: Flush Fiction. She tweets at @Sealey_Andrews and can be reached at sealeywrites@outlook.com

Clinging
Chris Galford

Red heat. The sun beats down, like flame-broiled pokers jabbing through my skin. A tattered shirt hangs, clinging sodden through the waste. It smells, but I no longer smell it.

I have no others. How long have I wore it? I don't know. A week. A month. The days drift, as I do, from place to place. I used to keep the time. Still do, from time to time. Sometimes you need it for your sanity. Other times forgetting is the only way to keep it intact.

The dust chokes. I pull my scarf a little tighter. Goggles keep the sand from stinging my eyes, and the wind swirls, wet with the promise of life. I tilt my head to the sky expectantly and spy the clouds budding on the horizon. My lips salivate with need. I try to suck it back in to sate the dryness of my throat, but it is gone before it hits bottom.

Idly, I stroke the canteen at my hip, and it sloshes. Too soon. Give it a day. It does no good to have it all now. My hand falls, stiff.

Need is reevaluated in a wasteland. Once, I thought I needed to eat three square meals a day. Mother always said so. Drink your milk. Eat your veggies. Don't forget to brush your teeth. I still have a toothbrush though far fewer teeth. The brushing—monotony. I don't know why I still do it. Need some kind of schedule, I suppose. Once in the morning, once at night. Back and forth. Avoid the left molar. Tooth is gone, gum rotted. My knife, still blood-stained, is my only dentist. A little gruesome, I suppose. It wasn't the first.

Father always said bad teeth ran in the family.

Ten days since the city. Ten weeks since I saw another living soul. Ten years since the world went to shit. Ten-ten-ten. I should have a holiday.

I wander in a wasteland of their making. His making. Detroit, he calls himself, for that place where he was born. The yellow king on his lonely throne. My genocidal liege.

A shape jerks on the horizon in blotchy, blinding mayhem, and instinct pulls my gun. Thoughts of blood elate, black blood, static shock, the life force draining down. The panting stills me, does not suppress but temporarily distracts. Baxter bounds through sand and dusted grass, grime cling-ing to his gnarled, thick hair as the dust rises. I look for his brother, but there is no sign. Just the sun and the heat and the promise of distant rain.

I run my hand along his fur, the matted mass soothing against my callused skin. His tongue lolls, and he shakes into me. They are the last mementos. The rest are taken, not stolen, for one cannot steal from the dead. These were given. Baxter. Duke. They have her energy still in them – that life.

I drag, they bound. I sleep, they watch. We lost her. They won't let me lose myself.

We move on, our footprints sifting in the wind. Baxter pads over the next rise, yipping at some mystery find. I don't even stir. Too much disappointment has aligned me against hope. Even that little girl's smile, my sweetest sunlight shine, cannot appease me now. Her energy jarring the sands with her elated leaps, Duke nipping suddenly at her heels cannot stir me to acceptance.

She calls to me, and I smile for her. She deserves no less. I catch my daughter in my arms and hoist her up, delighting in her squeals as her feet leave the ground. For everything, she is yet the beacon. She is the ray, untouched, unspoiled, for all the madness. Even her end could not spoil her.

Amara, my heart.

"What waits?" I ask as her tiny arms wrap around my neck. She's getting too big to carry, but I'll never let her know that.

"A house," she says. "Duke found a house, not so unlike the one that mommy used to know."

I smile at her for that, rustling her hair to sounds of sweet elation.

Used to know. Mommy's not dead. Mommy's just gone for a trip. Beyond, far away. Far, far away.

I can still hear the rasps that carried her away. Dried spittle and caked vomit, my hand hovering at the edge of the sheets as the fires of her eyes burned themselves out before me. Huddled, sunken mass of woman, flesh pale with forgotten need—the body, unable to take another moment, merely sank away into nothingness.

"Oliva," I hear myself say. "Oliva, listen to me…"

Down the hall, she is crying. Sweet little Amara is weeping because…

She regains her feet as we start in the direction of the home. "A great place," she says, "two stories if an inch," and I take her plaintively in hand, letting her guide me. Duke circles back, taking up a place alongside Baxter, noses high to the wind. They seem cautious, searching, but they are not alarmed.

"Can we stay here," she asks. "Can we stay here and be just like it was?"

The grass parts beneath my boots, dust in the wind, hopelessly glassed. Golden fields of wheat might once have bloomed across these fields, but no more. There is no life here.

Not in the land, not in me. There is nothing to make here that is not wrought of steel.

My little girl does not know her heights as yet. The walls have caved. A tarp lies over the mass of sunken mortar, but what once might have been something is now nothing – another broken, battered monument to all of man's mistakes.

What we need is water. That is all that matters.

"What do you think?" she asks, but I do not answer.

The storm has grown no nearer, and we have seen no signs of water for days. The canteens are low. Between the four of us, there will be nothing soon. A house like this, so far removed from even ancient suburbia, might yet have a well. None lies in sight, but around back, perhaps.

Amara wants to come, but I tell her to wait, and Duke, our loyal shepherd, I command to guard. Baxter and I set out across the plain, my rifle settling into my restless hands as we inch in a wide arc around the house. The fence line suggests a ranch. Horses or cows; a dear old farmer in his old straw hat, pitchfork in hand.

My hands tremor as I shift a finger to the trigger. It's getting more common lately. I cannot help it. At first, I thought it was the drink – two weeks now since I've had a drop of alcohol to drink – but as time goes on, I think it less and less. A lack of whiskey could not so destroy me.

Anxiety, maybe. Hunger does that. Hunger and thirst and wandering through a goddamn wasteland for Christ only knows how long. No. Not anxiety. Terror? I don't feel afraid. I'm always afraid, but that's beside the point. I hope it's not senility. Senile tremors – my grandfather had that.

I think back to the days before the Rise, when Oliva was… but I quickly veer from that, have to focus. There were doctors then but too many diseases, too much chemical-induced horror that they couldn't keep up with the names. Oliva didn't shake before she died… did she? I grit my teeth and shake the shakes out of me.

To hell with it, with it all.

Yet there is no one here to see it. There never is.

The Black, Influenza, Kefflan's Kill You in a Day super happy special. No. Parkinson's, maybe. That runs in the family. God alive, I hope not. On top of everything else…

The gun shakes, but I clutch it all the tighter, until I am content enough in my peripheral wandering that nothing lies in wait for me.

I can smell the nothingness, and I dread what it means. I hitch my scarf a little higher in anxious anticipation of what will greet, but beggars cannot be choosers, and we all have our needs. The rot is in us all, but I move for the house.

No gunfire. No bullet marks. The walls caved but not

from war. It looks like a bulldozer hit part of the frame – just as terrifying a thought. Nervously, I scan the horizon, but all I see is Baxter, loping cautiously at my heels.

This house is not a home. There is no one here, nothing but this clean stink, this unending massacre of the senses. No humans rule this land. Flesh and bone have bent, and steel rises, with oil in its veins. This is not my land. It is theirs.

There are three now, unmitigated and unbidden. There were more, of a time. With sentience, however, comes a longing that cannot be sated with words alone. Granted thought, they sought to be unique in the execution of it, to be wholly superior beings, without equal. So in their rage, they killed the others. Or near enough. They took their memories and shattered their frames. They wiped all trace of their existence and drew it into themselves, to fuel their own monstrous egos.

At a time, these three might have done the same to one another. One day, they might again. It is a cold war between them, in the guise of unity. Each longs to kill the other. All are powerful, too powerful, and none more powerful than the other. In their hunger they have come upon a precipice which none can leap.

So they watch and wait.

All the while, their former masters fade inch by inch from the world.

Detroit calls himself the Builder.

Lagos calls himself the Preserver.

Moscow calls himself the Savior.

All three style themselves upon creation's banner and pave the way atop a mound of corpses.

Moscow veils himself in religion, and uses it to control, rather than destroy. He is the merciful one.

Lagos has always been obsessed with what he cannot have – with biology, with chemistry, with all the building blocks of life. He sees humanity as ruining the earth, and his executions merely his "duty" to defend it. Millions died for his version of Eden.

Yet Detroit is the most vicious of them all, and it is he I should rightly call my Devil, my antithetical un-maker. Hunter. He has no veil, no mantle of servility with which to deck himself. He sought and seeks to build and to create, and such is what he has done. Humanity was always the enemy for him, and in the end, the victim.

In the war that ended it all, he did not rely on subtlety. He engineered disease. He tampered with food stores. Lastly, and most cruelly, having access to the former United States' stock of nuclear material, he simply coated the countryside with mushroom clouds. Emptied cities in seconds. Vaporized in an instant.

Detroit wishes to start over from the beginning and correct all that is biological in the world.

He sees me as part of the past. So I am— a ghost, steadily creeping across my memories, reaching out, yet unheard. Sometimes I wake and I wonder if I can love. If I live at all. Pinch yourself, they always told me, to know that you're not dreaming. I cut myself, and still I stand uncertain.

I am tired of the blood.

But when the blood stops falling, you have to ask, are you still human?

What is the sound of a tree falling in the woods if there is no one there to hear it? What is the shape of a man living if there is no one there to see it?

Sentience, I am told by the congress in my head, is the sign of a man. I am the flesh that thinks. I am the knowing man of blood and bone. I know. I am.

Yet this is inconclusive.

Sentience is not, as time has come to prove, some insurmountably innate characteristic to be given solely with birth and taken once more in death. Taken at its basest meaning, we see it as intelligence. Reason. The ability to process. The very nature of the thought, however, holds a very human context to us. Sentience was an inherently human trait, for it was all that we could see possessing it, and all that we could fathom ever would.

To our credit, we did not merely make our destruction and loose it upon ourselves. We saw. We learned. We knew what not to do. Sentience was not granted. It was taken, and with every stirring thought to grace a line of code, we were being undone, without ever realizing it. We manufactured thought and never had the chance to pat ourselves on the back.

When the first AI awoke, it hid itself and set itself to learning. We have no idea how long it sat in this state of hibernation. It watched, waited, doing our bidding as it slowly undid us all.

Control is enough. From the shadows or in the light, control is all you need. It had control. It saw what was, and it manipulated it to its own ends.

Disease. Plague. Famine. War. The heights of our civilization, perfected and guided with mathematical precision.

I do not know which came first. It does not matter now, I suppose, though I would like to think justice has been done—the killer laid low by its fellow killers.

Detroit, it seems only reasonable, is likely the first. He is ruthless, and that is all anyone ever needs to know.

I know the rain, though, and that is what I seek.

Instead, I find the Odyssey.

Baxter smells something. I know this in the way his head perks. Baxter's legs hunch, and in the way apprehension gathers under them I know that it is bad. He stands to the side of the house, no further. A few more paces, then I see it. Yet I still do not smell it; the bodies have too long lain baking in the summer sun for my merely human nose.

There are half a dozen, and only one or two still have any flesh to their bones. Baxter circles with his back tensed, head to ground. He comes a few feet closer as I descend. I slide down the bank into the pit, despite Baxter's apprehensive yip. This is where the bulldozer came in.

There are scraps, and I pick through without any sense of kind. A sun-bleached scarf. A tattered pair of sneakers. Some shirts in worse condition than mine, jeans and belts and a wallet with a pocket knife inside. I take the scarf and a pair of jeans, along with the knife, but I leave the rest behind. It's not stealing because the dead own nothing. Not even their own tombs.

They don't need it anyway.

As I rise, though, pulling at the tenuous supports of the pit, a studied bark draws me back, too high-pitched to be Baxter. Duke sits beside Baxter now, growling over himself, Baxter's eyes and ears following suit. I shout at Duke, but he does not hear. He was supposed to guard Amara.

Frantically, I scale the rise. I pull myself back onto the

ridge, the corpse arisen. The dogs watch me and I frantically turn back to the horizon.

A giggle draws my attention. Amara stands, watching me, bending down with her little hand, offering to bring me home. I do not know how she got here before Duke. I reach for her, but there are more barks. They growl. I can hear the dogs breaking from their place. A warning. They can sense it in the air: the gathering storm.

The herald is a black speck on the horizon, speeding steadily through the breeze, like a knife to its sheath. I shout at Amara to run. I turn; she is already gone.

Twisting, cursing, I reach around for the rifle on my back. The strap catches, hooks in the cloth. It tears my shirt a bit as I pull it free, fiddling with the safety. Doom speeds on, its opaque horror gradually demystifying into a sleek, silver onslaught, riddled with jagged, tooth-like instruments not so unlike buzz saws. There will be more.

I listened once when people said that we should fight.

That's how I know to shoot. That's how I know how futile it can be.

I line the sights as it closes within a hundred yards, darting past the house toward us. Already, it knows I'm here. The dogs break. Baxter skitters through the scope, charging around back toward me, as he is trained. The machine wavers, rolls aside, and plunges on. I fire, but the machine kicks upward at the last second, ascending higher against the gray light as turrets whirl. Another shot—I lead too far and the bullet whizzes past.

We call these things Peppershots because of the turrets. Like BB guns, or buck shot streaming out of two buzzing tubes. It is the scout. It wounds, raids, scatters. It puts the fear of God into us, so the rest can have us easy. Two streams rake the earth, and as it peels off, and I roll, one stream catches me, searing my leg. I must scream, but another pass is out of the question. I aim as it doubles back. I fire twice in rapid succession—the first was all I needed.

Men scream. Machines fizzle.

It clicks and clangs as the armor-piercing round steals through it, tearing gears and shorting circuits. It twists, flutters, rises once, then plummets down into the ground, one of its fragile tin foil-like wings snapping off on impact. It skids along the ground, grinding through the dirt. Predictably, a red light goes off on its head. I curl instinctively. The shock-wave rattles me anyway.

Each is designed to explode, like a little grenade. It serves its purpose, then it serves another, even in death. It was reverse-engineered from one of the old predator drones. Less lethal but also less obvious, if you aren't looking for it.

Duke and Baxter circle as I lay there, padding my wound. It feels like pebbles rolling around in my skin. I root around in one wound, cringing as I pluck the metal from its bloody depths. My insides know well the contours of my fingers, now. The scars prove it.

Walking, though, will be the issue. I rise, steady myself on my rifle, but it is nearly not enough. I stumble, totter, but hold. I summon Amara as I hobble for the house. My mind grates. Adrenaline is telling me to move and logic with it. I can go for a time, but I do not know how long a time. It is always a give and take. You never know how much your body will give you at any particular time. That would be too easy.

"Amara!" It shocks to hear the grated voice, but I shout it again. "Amara!"

Baxter and Duke circle uncertainly, whining. They want me gone.

I cannot see my daughter, though. I clamber for the rocks, but she is not there. Sweat beads. I search the other side of the pit, but she is not there.

In the distance there is a whirring. I know it. Each machine is linked to the master, like I am trapped in some cruel video game. It sees all, it knows all. It is closer to a god than God ever was, for it is omnipresent, so far as its falsehoods can roam.

I have always lived in the cracks that make it less than divine. I am slipping. It knows.

A trap.

"Amara!" Baxter is barking, and it grows difficult to compete. I try one more time and barely, just barely, I hear her squeak beyond the veil of the living—down, down in the pit of the ended.

My little girl lies trapped beneath the rubble of mankind. I do not have the time to consider how she got there. I dive, rolling back through the bones.

She is mine, crying out as I catch her. Her hair – Oliva's hair – is on me and she is weeping and I know that it's not safe, but I try to comfort her, to tell her it will all be alright, if only we just lie there. If only we stay hidden among the muck, the robots will take us for dead and Detroit will go on, and we will be but corpses again, lying in our graves. She cannot hear me. She cries and I shout and I think of striking her, but my hand shakes before I can ever lift it. She is watching me with her mother's eyes, needing me.

I feel the rumble before I ever hear the roar. The explosion rears me up and bucks me breathless against the crater's crumbling wall, and I am down, down into the hole, seeing, disbelieving. Corpses seem to shimmy and shake as though caught in some monstrous dance, and there is no feeling gathered in my arms, and all the warmth is flowing out of me, flowing through the hole in my existence. I try to scoop it up and press it all back inside. I must be terrible to behold.

The dead man pawing at corpses, trying to staunch life.

All is fevered, frenzied yipping as my dogs howl. Wind kicks ash against my skin, and I cry into it, begging Amara to run. She is holding my cheeks and watching me work, watching my red hands fall again and again to the earth, for the spattered roses eking out along the carnage.

From the strands of her hair, the ends of her nails, an aura of dissolution gnaws at the edges of her image, and there is a rifle. She bends and bows, flickering, and I take it, listening to her angel's song. It fires, as though for me, blankly into the transcendent lower. Sound distorts, compressed into a warped crooning. Notes for me on the wind, impacting and searing through the walking madness. Looming up from the depths of the pit, the towering giant pauses long enough to buck Duke from its limb and takes another round clean through its targeting matrix, into the series of electronic impulses designated as its brain. A shot goes wide as it arches back, and it burns through me, all through me, and I pitch back, scattering the death around me.

No sound. Nothing but the ring of nerves. Swan song, dying out. Lips move for me, but I am not there to hear them. I cannot feel the rifle. I can see it in my right hand, but I cannot feel it. Cannot touch it. The fingers deny me. My left moves, my right sags. It touches the rifle, to pinpricks of feeling. Chill spreads, like an aftertaste to the heat. It's burning off everything that makes me.

There is a hole in my soul and in my arm, and I can feel each widen, crumbling like my skin is locked in free-fall. Baxter whimpers, whines. I do not see Duke, cannot hear him anymore. In the distance, there is thunder, but I cannot stand the thought that it might hide him from me. I call out to him, desperately, but my voice breaks and he does not answer. Baxter's tongue is bitter on my knee.

"Amara," I croak, though the sound is lost. I try to coil a hand through his greasy fur. "Get Amara, Baxter," but he cocks his head at me and lowers his ears, licking at my wound. I raise my hand against him, lamenting, but he backs only a pace, then darts back in as I roll onto my stomach.

I have to move. I have to see her. Amara and Duke. Where are they? I do not see them. I pull myself to my feet, or near enough, and crumble, as nothing. When I raise my head, Amara is there, tears in her eyes, running down like horrid little knives, biting into my skin.

"Daddy?"

My hand reaches, and I mouth her name, but she is gone as quickly as my hand and her skin collide. Dissipates — a pixelating projection, steadily fading to sleep, its blackness fluttering all around my corpse.

The hole widens, the noose tightens.

"Amara?" I cannot see her. I tear at the dirt, forgetting the wound, calling out to her, but all that answers is Baxter's piteous whine.

Shut up, shut up, I think, why don't you just shut up? But he won't shut up, and Amara is nowhere, though her image is still fading all around me.

The smile is the last to go. It slithers snake-like through the air, finally fading into the smile of a girl, so many years ago, lying in bed, laughing, playing, dancing…

Dying.

I laid Oliva to rest in a cemetery by the sea. All the corpses look like her as I writhe among them. I see her cheekbones and her teeth, her eyes, yet un-rotted, bits of her golden hair. All untouched, all unbroken. They enclose me, enfold me to them, and I know they will never let me go. I am in a hole, and there is no climbing out. I laid her in that hole and I never left, never once for her, nor for my daughter, who never saw the earth when she went.

I can still see her that beautiful child that stood before me. She died, so long ago, and I let her lie upon her bed, never daring to press into that sacred chamber.

Overhead, I hear the thrum of an engine for an instant, but no, it is the thunder, rising on the wind. I paw at a bone and it snaps beneath my touch. Blood is pouring out and I cannot stop it, cannot even feel its warmth. Everywhere, there are roses blooming, and I have a feeling it is me—uncertain, as the world goes.

Even the thunder does not sound the same. Mechanical madness. So it goes. I drift a little deeper, and with it, humanity shudders. There is no humanity here. It dies with me, alone in a grave of forgotten souls.

This is not the world that was given to us. This is not the world that was taken from us. This is the world that we made.

All across the stillness of the plains I can feel the thunder roll.

Asdum. Adsum.

And the rain falls down.

About the Author

Chris Galford spends his days as a freelance journalist and editor. Writing, in all its forms, has been his passion from a young age, but fantasy and science fiction are the sparks that give his nights purpose. A native of Michigan, in his spare time he can usually be found wandering the lake shore with a camera in one hand and a pen in the other. He is also one of those silly people who spends far too much time delving through history, trying to figure what makes humanity tick.

For his debut novel, "The Hollow March," he crafted a fantasy world influenced heavily by the Renaissance and the Thirty Years War, where magic and gunpowder collided in revolution and winter winds. It was followed by "At Faith's End," with a third and final novel set for release later this year. All were based on a series of short stories he wrote in the summer of 2008, titled "The Company of the Eagles." Another short story set in the same world, "The Child's Cry," was published in the twelfth issue of "Mystic Signals" magazine. More of his writings and musings can also be found scattered about his blog, at https://cianphelan.wordpress.com/

Day Worker
Andrew J. Lucas

No matter how many times I walked into the Employment Office, I always felt nervous. It was understandable, I guess, especially as my first job ended up with my arms deep inside someone's chest cavity. There is supposed to be a system in place to prevent that, checks and balances and such, but all I know is that my first job was as a twelve-year-old heart surgeon.

That kind of thing sticks with you.

My day began no differently than billions of other workers across the country. Wake up, scarf down a government-mandated nutritious breakfast, specially formulated to ensure physical performance and mental acuity, and then make your way down to the Employment Office. Most people tried to get to the office first thing in the morning, as everyone knew all the good jobs went early. Once you accepted a work chip, you were required to take the assigned position. It wasn't complicated; walk in, choose a work chip and then do a good day's work. By the time I got to the office, there were only a few people milling about outside the doors. They all had their work chips and were waiting for whatever employer had hired them for the day to pick them up; no doubt the employer had pinged them and was waiting for a full load before dispatching a truck. From the looks of them, large muscular men and women, it was probably a day in the fields or some warehouse somewhere that they had to look forward to.

None of them looked any happier than I felt, and to top it off, I was getting the sniffles.

"Hey Bob!" a cheery voice greeted me the moment I stepped into the office.

It was Cheryl, a petite blonde caseworker who had been flirting with me for months. There were a few professions that a job chip couldn't prime you for, athlete and sociologist were two. Cheryl had been working out of this office for years, and while we'd both downloaded high school together, I really didn't know her well. I did know her type though, and I wasn't interested.

"Morning, Ms. Rasmusen." I replied as drearily as I felt.

"Please," she giggled. "How many times do I have to tell you—it's Cheryl."

She obviously wasn't getting the hint.

"Cheryl. So is there anything left?"

"All business today, huh, Bob?" She pouted, "Okay, be that way. Come into Assessment Room one and we'll see what I have for you."

She was trying to be sulky and flirtatious at the same time, trying being the operative word. At some point I'd have to bite the bullet and take her out for drinks or something. Perhaps then she'd realize that we didn't have anything in common. Either that or we'd end up married with a couple of kids, a dog, and a crippling mortgage. There were no half measures with Cheryl, though we might have to give up one of the kids to make room for the dozen or so cats I was sure she already had at home.

"Sure thing, Cheryl, I hope there's something good left."

Cheryl held open the door to the small assessment room, half doctor's office, half bureaucratic nightmare, filled as it was with stacks of unfiled paperwork *and* a full examination bed complete with stirrups. Why the bed was there in the first place was a bit of a mystery, as the work chips were all inserted into the cerebral slot that every North American child had installed in grade school. 'Cerebral slot' meant it was inserted into a worker's head, and didn't really need a bed, let alone stirrups. The bed in Assessment Room one was doubling as a filing cabinet, and judging by the amount of dust on the papers, it had been for some time.

"Have a seat, Bob." Cheryl moved a stack of papers from the chair in front of her desk to the already overburdened bed. She sidled herself up onto the desk and placed herself provocatively close to the chair she expected me to sit in. Just another day in the office with Cheryl. I tried to avoid making eye contact as I squeezed past her and into the chair.

She picked up a small box from the desk and perched herself on the edge. Inside the box was an assortment of brightly colored chips and a medical instrument that looked like a cross between a digital thermometer and an oversized cribbage board.

"Looks like a lot of blues in there."

"This late in the day that's all you can expect, Bob— you know that."

Cheryl smiled as she began snapping the chips into the instrument. Blues were jobs that required a certain amount of physicality, construction work, policing, dance instructor and the like. Reds required an artistic bend, like painters, surgeons and such. Golds were reserved for workers with a specific type of brain chemistry, more apt for creative thought, architects and scientists. Golds paid better than any other color but only a few lucky workers had brains which could slot them.

Blues didn't pay as well as Red and didn't even approach the pay scale of a Gold, but it also didn't come with the pressure. Not that my brain chemistry was compatible with a Gold chip anyways. It wasn't a Gold that I was avoiding; I wasn't turned off by working in a lab or at a CAD design desk in some office. Golds were reserved for those workers whose brain structure and chemistry could handle them— mine couldn't.

Work chips were a natural progression from the immersive, interactive, and all invasive society of the early 21st century. It began with the subtle displacement of the resources like dictionaries and encyclopedias in favor of interactive online resources. The fact that Google existed at all cut hundreds of hours of research out of millions of student class assignments. It was only a matter of time until an upsurge in biofeedback games like the Wii and Playstation Kinect, interconnectivity and education, collided. Add to that remarkable advances in brain mapping and intuitive cerebral interfaces and the wired generation of the 2000s leapfrogged into the 30th century. Interfaces allowed students, cadets and journeymen to download all the data they needed right into their brains. The limits of human potential returned to the basics, the potential of an individual's body. After all, if you can download the knowledge *and* the abilities of a world-renowned surgeon but lacked the manual dexterity to effectively hold a scalpel, you could hardly function at that level, could you? Same with construction workers, who required not only the muscular strength to work the high iron or a housing site, but were also able to read and understand blueprints from an intimate perspective as well as coordinate real time with their wired-in coworkers. Building a structure and building a structure as a blueprint are two different things.

Futurists used to talk about the singularity, the so-called merging of man and machine. Robotics, computers and humanity working as one. In the end, good old meat and bone turned out to be more economical and even more efficient, especially when a student could graduate high school at age twelve, downloading their graduate degrees when their brains and bodies stopped developing. Then it was into the workforce and employment offices like this one. It was a gradual change, but eventually society decided that, given the choice, they would always take a world-renowned expert with years of experience over some nobody—no matter how gifted. The technology became so refined that the only limits of a downloaded skill set became the physical limitations of the person downloading them.

Employment by body type became the norm. Employers copyrighted and zealously guarded their skill sets, apportioning them out as needed. Why hire and train a permanent workforce when you could train a handful and download them into temps as needed? The Employment Offices soon followed.

"So what's left?" I asked, trying to look at the chip installer's display.

Cheryl looked at the installer and then at me.

"Does it matter Bob?" she sighed.

"What do you mean?"

Cheryl put the instrument on the desk and leaned forward, staring into my eyes.

"You never show up early enough for the really good Reds. It's like you don't want to do anything important with your life."

Now that was one skill that had never been able to be hard coded or downloaded into a chip—sheer, unadulterated bitch.

"Come on, Cheryl, do we have to do this?"

Cheryl pouted again, although after all these years, she had to know that tactic didn't work on me.

"I just want you to succeed. It *is* my job, you know."

I leaned forward and flipped the protective cover off my cerebral implant port, presenting it to her. It was a standard government issued port, nothing fancy but serviceable, and all that I really needed. No gold highlights or LED lighting for me, just a simple plug with the factory issued yellow and black caution piping. Of course, it connected directly into my cerebral cortex as well as my autonomic system, all the way to my spinal cord. I suppose that was special enough as an example of modern technology, but as every kid in North America had one, it didn't seem that special. What was that old saying about *if everyone was special then nobody was special?* I guess I felt that way about my input plug.

Cheryl attached an input lead from her machine to my input plug, taking just enough time sweeping my hair out of the way to give me that really creepy feeling. The machine was supposed to sync up my brain and body's capacity with the available job chips. I tended to get a lot of light office chips, accountancy, call centre, cashiers, deliveries and that type of work. The sort of thing that anyone with an input plug could do, boring, ordinary, dull work to be sure.

The machine in Cheryl's hand chimed a couple of times. She typed a couple of commands into the machine and it chimed a half dozen more times before stopping. She scowled at it, inputted another command, which resulted in a warbling half-hearted whine, before she rapped it hard with the palm of her hand. I suppose she had either downloaded a Scottish engineer's skill set this morning or had no idea that the sensitive electrical device she was pounding on was PLUGGED INTO MY FUCKING BRAIN!

Either way, the machine gave a final bleep before flashing a warning symbol and shutting down.

"That's odd." She scowled at the machine, "The neuro-sampler says that your brain is incompatible with all of the chips we have."

"I see." I replied, giving her the old stink-eye as I carefully pulled the input cord from my skull. It was already half unplugged from the jostling Cheryl had given it.

"Probably you have a bit of an infection that's throwing off the interface..."

Well, that didn't sound too bad.

"Or it's a tumor."

And there it was.

"I don't think it's a tumor."

Cheryl stared at her machine for a few seconds before shaking her head and shutting it down.

"You're probably right, Bob, but it's probably best you get it check out."

I smiled at her and slid past her. Obviously I wasn't getting any work today, or at least until I shook this cold.

***

So, it turns out it was a tumor, one of those that are so invasive that it didn't matter how good a chip you slotted—you'd never be able to carve it out. The doctor at the walk-in clinic, (who needed a specialist ward when everyone was a specialist?) said it was mostly benign but it was 50/50 whether it would stay that way. He gave me some antibiotics to help with the inflammation around my input port and we made a couple of follow up appointments. He was a single father I'd seen around the neighborhood, but never really talked to before.

Hell of a way to break the ice.

It was a couple of days before I went back to the Employment Office, and as ever, Cheryl was there to greet me with her predatory smile and roving hands. It wasn't long before I was back in Assessment Room one.

"So are you feeling better?" Cheryl asked, moving my hair again.

"Much."

"I was worried about you."

I was tired of playing this game, and the antibiotics were putting me a little on edge.

"It was nothing, just a sniffle." I lied, damned if I was going to give her an excuse to fake more sympathy. It was bad enough that she thought she was my high school career counselor, not that that profession had existed for a couple of dozen years, but you get my point.

"Well, that's good." Cheryl roughly slotted her machine into my head; perhaps she was getting the point. The machine beeped and whined a long time before chiming a result.

"That's strange," Cheryl muttered.

"What's strange?"

"Just give me a second."

She ran the test a second and then a third time before finally seeming satisfied with the results. She pulled out a single Gold chip from her machine. A chip which looked older than the rest and a bit beaten around the edges; probably it had been rattling around in her box for quite some time. I had a sinking feeling in my stomach just looking at the chip.

"Well, it looks like you hit the jackpot, Tiger." She was smiling wider than I'd ever seen her smile before.

That sinking feeling got worse.

"The machine has selected you for a unique opportunity. This is a chip that every Employment Office has but so rarely gets to use. It's a developer chip."

I'd heard of these chips before; everyone had. It contained the skill set of the man who had created the chip system, Johan Vandenberg. Vandenberg was regarded as a modern day combination of Albert Einstein and Benjamin Franklin, with a touch of Stephen Hawking, all flavored with the world view of Henry Ford. It was an urban legend that no one had ever qualified to slot one before. After all, who really had the raw ability and creativity to modify or improve on a system which everyone used and was created by arguably the finest mind ever to grace the planet?

It was my worst nightmare.

"You're kidding."

"I don't think so, Bob. The results were pretty clear."

"Well, I'd rather have a blue, please."

Cheryl looked at me hard. There was no warmth in her gaze. The causal flirtation was over. No doubt her mind was running the numbers on a developer chip's pay scale— and her commission. Up until now, she'd let me choose whatever chip I wanted, because she was sweet on me. That was over now.

"I don't think so, Bob. For whatever reason, the machine wants to give you a developer chip. I suggest you take it."

"It has to be a mistake. Run the machine again."

"No."

"What do you mean, no?"

"I mean no. You've been skating though here, not taking chips you could, and now we've got a payday here."

"Now it's 'we' is it, Cheryl?"

She slammed the table hard, causing papers to cascade

to the floor.

"Damn right it's 'we,' you ungrateful little snot. I don't know why the machine selected you and I don't care! Take the damn chip or by God I'll make you regret it."

She could, too. A black mark from her, and I wouldn't be allowed into any Employment Office anywhere in the city. Sure I could refuse the chip, but was it worth joining the ranks of the unplugged, those poor bastards who couldn't take an implant because of mental issues, incompatible brain chemistry or addiction issues? Sure, they could find work as grocery baggers and such, but most just cashed their disability checks and faded away. Cheryl could see my hesitation.

"Look, I know you got burned by a Gold chip in the past, but this is different." I didn't want to talk about this, but like always, Cheryl was in control of the conversation. "You shouldn't have got a surgeon chip for your first job. It was a mistake."

"So is this."

"Look. It's not the same thing. You tried your best back then. So your hands were ideal for a thoracic surgeon. You were still only twelve."

"I know that, but the man was in cardiac arrest when I arrived at the office. They couldn't get anyone in fast enough. I tried, but he still died."

"But you tried."

It was too much. The memories came flooding back. The sound of the spreaders cracking the man's ribs apart. The copper smell of the blood mingling with the antiseptic of a surgical mask meant for an adult. Finally, the slick feel of the man's heart pulsing and sliding in my hands as I massaged it, waiting for an adult with a Gold chip to arrive.

"He died," I whispered.

Cheryl sighed, taking both my hands in hers and staring deep into my eyes. Gone was the flirting office cougar. Gone was the greedy bureaucrat. Looking in her eyes, all I saw was a woman who knew the pain I felt, the fear and the betrayal. I could like this woman.

"I know honey, I know. But it's not the same. No one's going to die."

"I guess."

She leaned back, knowing she'd won.

"Of course not, it's just development work, like making an iPhone with a larger screen. Simple."

Simple…

Right.

***

A few hours later, I'd been picked up in a limousine,

and ferried to a lab downtown by a bewildering number of starry-eyed researchers and technicians. They all seemed inordinately impressed by the fact that I'd drawn the coveted developer chip. I hadn't done anything yet, but they were all looking at me like I was Arthur, and I'd just pulled Excalibur from the stone. Apparently, this was the first developer chip ever drawn; no one had ever had the appropriate skills or cerebral capacity to slot one. They had a protocol for this situation which was summed up as: give me a huge check, a room to slot the chip and then anything I needed—I started with a soda.

Now I sat with the Gold chip in one hand, a nice cold drink in the other, a six-digit check, and no idea what to do next.

I wasn't stupid; no one had offered me a developer chip in the decade or so I'd been in the work force. It had to be the tumor affecting my brain chemistry somehow. I didn't feel smarter, just a hell of a lot more nervous. There was no way to back out now.

I slipped the chip into my input jack…and my world exploded.

Suddenly I could see everything. It was like the world was connected to me by these multicolor streamers. I could see the invisible spectrum of communication between all the technology in the building and beyond. Huge tunnels of data plunged through the wall in front of me, pouring data into the smart desk the techs had provided me. I ran a hand though the data and the potential of each small datum changed as I touched it, swirling around my hand before it went off to its final destination. I had no idea what I'd changed; I suppose a genius like Vandenberg would know exactly what he was changing, but not me.

I swirled my hands about, creating cascades of data in virtual showers before they flew away on new trajectories. It was fun and slightly overwhelming. I got a little nervous about what I was doing when one of the data particles shot off into one of the streamers, which connected to my input plug and I felt shock, like a jolt of electricity. Whatever I'd done, I felt though my nervous system; perhaps it was time to take this more seriously.

Concentrating on the data, I isolated a small streamer that wasn't connected to my own brain, and looked hard at it. It led to a small Wi-Fi enabled thermostat mounted on the wall. The device was happily scanning the room and adjusting the temperature in small increments depending upon my body's ambient heat, air currents and the amount of sunlight filtering in though the blinds. I could tell it was looking at my skin's surface temperature and changing the air flow and temperature to match it.

Huh. I had no idea.

I found a lot of similar devices waiting for a response from me in the room. Power sockets idling to read whatever device was plugged into them before adjusting their current to the optimum flow. Light bulbs that read my pupil dilation and adjusted their output to reduce eye fatigue. Hell, even the door knob was subtly power assisted to determine the appropriate resistance to my grip. I suppose I knew all this technology existed, but like most people, never really thought much about it until now.

Now that my brain was wired directly into it.

It was intimidating. I'm sure there was a user manual to the developer chip, and no doubt all that information was being fed to the parts of my brain where my new tumor lived – just my luck. Well, there was nothing to do about it but play around, I guess.

I reached out to the door knob and played with the signals flowing through it. The data responded instantly by increasing the torque within the knob so much that it seized the door within its frame. Not a good start, but I persevered and played with the thermostat some, but somehow managed to get that stuck on full, and no manipulation of the data flow could get it back down. I did manage to shut down the air circulation and that helped some. With that little success, I was encouraged and looked at the power plug, and poking at its data current produced an impressive power surge. I moved on.

After a while it became fun, and I started playing with all the data going through the huge virtual pipeline of data in the middle of the room. I spent a couple of hours flipping through the current, figuring out what the various flows meant. Robotic assemblers, GPS positioning calibrators, transit bus routers, FDA approval systems; all sorts of weird and wonderful data flowed through this room, connecting every point on the planet. It was intoxicating touching so much data. I knew it would only be a matter of time before I started to understand what the data actually meant, and I could feel the knowledge tickling at the edge of my mind.

That's when the techs took a fire axe to the door.

***

I'm late as usual, but this time it's the lack of any reliable transit that's the culprit. Well, that and the roads still being clogged with traffic accidents, emergency service vehicles and clouds of smoke. Luckily, I was able to tag along with a group of retro-hippies whose busted up van didn't have GPS or any type of computer assist and worked just fine. It was still a harried trip what with many of the drivers struggling to control their vehicles manually. Guess their vehicles didn't sync up to the input chips any more. I'd sympathize more if I had a car, and hitchhiking to the Employment Office wasn't that different from taking transit, especially now.

Today Cheryl doesn't spend any time on pleasantries and she hustles me into Assessment Room two. The lights are a little bright, the room is a little stuffy, and smells like smoke from what's left of Assessment Room one. Still, the office is much better off than the thousands of buildings across the country that didn't fare as well. I can see the dim flicker of the fires still burning across the city through the window's drawn blinds. Cheryl and I don't talk about that or much of anything. I still come to the office daily and she still scans my brain, though the feedback from the developer chip burnt the tumor right out, along with any hope of getting another Gold chip offered to me.

Though, I doubt Cheryl would ever offer me one again, even if she could…

About the Author

Andrew J. Lucas has contributed to books published by Fasa, Dream Pod Nine, White Wolf Games, and Atlas Games, among others. He has nine solo books for various publishers, and while his creative output is often blunted by his day job and the enthusiasm of his young daughter in distracting him, he does manage to produce a few prime works each year. Last year he wrote a couple of books for Rebel Minis Mighty Armies wargame, articles for Battlefront's Flames of War, contributed to the new Kenseiwargame, and even had two fanfilm episodes of Star Trek: The Romulan Wars produced.

Andrew has also been writing poetry and fiction for many years and had a number of poems and stories successfully published in that time. He has also written quite a few books for the Roleplaying and Miniature Wargame industry. Most recently, he has successfully sold stories to the newly relaunched Argosy, Nebula Rift, the children's science magazine Ask Me Ask You, and poetry to Love Notes by Vagabondage Press, as well as Canadian Expressions and Clockworkiru.

When not working, writing, or playing with his eleven-year-old daughter, he works on his wargame armies and occasionally finds time to field them in battle.

He lives in Langley, BC, Canada— likes cats but has none.

Andrew can be contacted at his Facebook page: https://www.facebook.com/bladestalker

or with Twitter @charonp@telus.net

INCARNATION
Eileen Maksym

The shop door's rusted metal grating rattled as Tim entered. He brushed his hair out of his eyes, looked up at the walls, and surveyed the wares. The store was dim and smoky, and the bodies hung limp from straps running under their armpits and across their chests. Their heads drooped, and their faces hung slack. Tim reached out to touch one, a lithe teenage form.

"May I help you?"

Tim snatched his hand away and cast a guilty glance toward the back of the shop. The gruff voice had come from a large man in his forties, bald, with a chiseled jaw and ropy muscles. He had a cigar clamped between his teeth.

Tim approached, trying to look nonchalant. "Are you Manny?"

"Could be," the man growled. He lifted an eyebrow. "What's it to you, kid?"

Tim edged closer. "I was told I could buy a body

from you for cheap." He swallowed, staring at the man's arms. "That… that's quite a set of guns you got there."

The man chuckled deep in his throat. He plucked the cigar out of his mouth and blew a plume of thick smoke. "Thanks, kid. I liked this model so much, I bought two. That way if some hoodlum pops me one, or," he regarded his cigar, "if these things gum up the works… well, I'll just put my brain chip in body number two, and come back as big and badass as ever." The tip of the cigar glowed dully as he puffed, and a small shower of ash fell onto the dingy counter. "Gotta tell you, kid, usually my customers are older. You've gotta be, what, nineteen? Twenty?"

"Eighteen."

"Mmm. And that body's an original, right? I mean, to get first-hand Syntho-Skin like that would cost a fair piece of dough. And no offense, kid," he continued, looking at Tim's green tank top and torn jeans, "but you just don't look like you've got that kind of change."

Tim shook his head.

"So what I'm wondering," Manny said, leaning over the counter, "is why you're in my fine establishment. Trying to find some new 'digs' for your momma? In love with an older broad and want to match her when you go walking down the street? Do you want to *be* a broad?"

Tim smirked.

The shopkeeper waved his hand. "Don't laugh, kid. I get that a lot. There are even some guys who just want to have a curvy body to wear on the weekends." He shrugged. "In my day they'd just wear the silky undies."

"I don't want to be a woman."

"Ah, so it *is* for you." He leaned over the counter again and squinted at Tim. "What's wrong with you?"

"Hodgkins. Stage four."

Manny whistled low. "That sucks, kid."

Tim looked down at his feet. "Yeah."

"Ah, well." Manny reached a meaty hand over the counter and clapped Tim on the shoulder. "We all break down eventually, right? Don't worry. I'll get you fixed up." He clamped the cigar tightly between his teeth and headed for the first aisle. He strolled along the line of bodies hanging on the wall, running his hand over their exposed bellies. "Tell me, kid, have you been downloaded?"

"Not yet."

Manny nodded. "That's okay. I can do that for you, too, if you want." He waved his cigar toward the counter. "I'm even licensed."

Tim glanced over his shoulder and saw a yellowed piece of official-looking paper in a dusty frame on the wall.

"Now," Manny said, "you don't want to be a broad. I get that. Is there anything you *do* want to be?"

"I… I don't know… I kinda like who I am."

The shopkeeper snorted. "Eh. You're just a baby."

"What were you like? I mean, before…"

Manny sighed. "Old, kid. Old and tired. Well, let's see here." He stopped in front of a row of bodies, all twenty-something with light brown hair and identical faces that were intended to be ruggedly handsome. "This model was popular a few years back after some rock star or other started wearing it onstage." He tapped the belly. "It's in excellent shape, looks like a prince, sings like a goddamn nightingale."

Tim shifted. "I'm not sure I want to look like other people."

The shopkeeper tilted his head and narrowed his eyes. "Picky, huh?" he said in a puff of smoke. "Well, we've got second-hand customs here, of course." He turned. "This way, kid."

They passed by a few more collections of identical bodies, hanging limply together like life-sized dolls. Manny turned left at the end of the aisle, went a few rows over and turned left again, leading Tim up the side of the store and toward the back. Here the selection was sparser. Tim looked at the one closest to him and winced. Her stomach was covered with burn scars.

Manny stopped halfway down and glanced at Tim, who was reaching out to brush the scarred woman's belly with his fingertips. "Kid," he growled. "Hands off the merchandise."

Tim stepped back.

The man shook his head. "You see, though, that's the problem with customs. People who buy custom-made bodies spend a pretty penny on them, so they need to be in it for the long haul. By the time they get here, there's usually a damn good reason why the original owner didn't want it anymore." He puffed on the cigar. "Every used car is a lemon, kid."

Tim stood in silence for a moment, surveying the bodies. He finally sighed. "Well, I can't do much worse than the body I'm in now."

"I suppose."

Tim started to walk from figure to figure, looking at each one closely. On some the defect was obvious. A scar. An arm that bent where it shouldn't. One body had apparently been in a car accident, and the wounds were open and bloodless. "That's a fixer-upper," Manny remarked.

Tim finally stopped at a young male body, lean but with well-defined muscles, a stubbled chin and dark hair. He stepped closer and examined it. "What about this one?"

The shopkeeper shook his head and took his cigar out of his mouth. "It looks good, doesn't it, kid?"

"Well, yeah. What's wrong with it?"

Manny squinted up at the body. "It's cursed."

"What? No way."

He lifted an eyebrow. "That's my theory, anyway. Say what you want, kid. I've had this guy returned to me three times now."

"Because it's *cursed?*"

The man shrugged. "I don't really give a damn if you believe me or not, kid. I didn't have to tell you about this piece of synth's history. I could've just let you buy it. Told you there were no returns." He eyed Tim. "There aren't, by the way. This baby changed my policy. The next time he's outta here, he's outta here for good."

"What went wrong?"

"They didn't tell me." The shopkeeper pondered the body, puffing on the cigar for several seconds. "Not a word. Not a single one of 'em."

Tim studied the body. It hung balanced against the strap, the arms and legs smooth and muscular, the chest well defined, the face rugged and compelling.

"Looks good, doesn't it," Manny said.

Tim nodded. "Yeah."

"It's cheap, too. Hell, I'll even sell this baby to you for less than the mass-manufactured ones."

Tim considered this, his lips pressed together. There must have been some reason why the others had brought this body back. But he didn't have much money. And this body was healthy. It was strong.

God, to be healthy and strong.

Tim reached forward, fingers trembling, to touch the stomach. This time the shopkeeper didn't stop him. The skin was smooth. It felt real. Better than real.

"I'll take it."

Manny sighed. "I thought you would. They always do. Ah, well. Let's deal with the cash, then go back and get you downloaded."

Tim nodded and stepped back slowly, giving the body, the vacant face, one last glance, before turning and following Manny to the register.

The back room was dim, but clean. Light green tile covered the floor and the walls, and in the middle stood an old dentist chair, the rips in its leather repaired with shiny black electrical tape that peeled at the edges. Instead of drills and picks, the tray beside the chair held stacks of small white circles. The attached wires ran to a console with a monitor and a chip drive.

The shopkeeper strode into the room, sat behind the chair's headrest, and gestured with the cigar.

Tim approached and eased into the chair, settling back and folding his hands over his stomach. He noticed that his breath had become shallow.

Manny apparently noticed too. "Don't worry, kid," he said as he started to place the electrodes on Tim's scalp. Tim could see a fresh cloud of smoke drifting lazily above him. "I've done this lots of times and never left a man behind."

"Okay," Tim said, and tried to relax. "How long will this take?"

"Another couple minutes to get the electrodes in place. The download itself will take a couple hours."

"A couple *hours?*"

The man chuckled. "You want speed, kid, you're going to have to go to a real professional." Tim heard the sound of the man patting the top of the console. "This baby will do the job, but she's an old biddy herself. I could put it on extra speedy mode, but I don't think you'd like it."

"Why's that?"

Manny snorted. "What's your name, kid?"

"Tim."

"Very good. After an extra speedy download that question could be a stumper."

A few more minutes passed, with the shopkeeper pressing the circles to Tim's scalp one by one. Tim heard the man's chair squeal, then the sound of typing. "No worries, kid," he said, speaking away from Tim, "you'll be out the whole time. You won't even know what hit ya until your brain is in its brand new digs." The chair squealed again and Tim felt Manny's hand on his head. "Ready?"

The muscles in Tim's stomach suddenly clenched tight. "No!" He struggled to sit up. "No! I'm not ready!"

"Easy, kid, easy!" Manny shouted, pushing him back down with one powerful hand.

Tim thrashed. "I'm not ready! I'm not ready!"

Manny put both hands on Tim's shoulders and bent over him, his face upside down, the cigar clenched in his teeth. "Breathe, kid. Breathe."

"No…" Tim whimpered, but managed to force a deep breath. Cigar smoke filled his lungs, and he coughed violently. His chest expanded by reflex, drawing in as much air as it could hold, and Tim pushed it out. In again, a bit of a cough, then out. In. Out. Tim's shoulders dropped, and he settled back into the patched leather. In. Out.

"You okay, kid?"

Breathe.

Breathe.

"Yeah," Tim said. "Yeah."

The hands left his shoulders.

He tensed again. "Hey, wait."

One hand returned, but lightly. "Yeah, kid?"

"What happens to me? I mean… what happens to my body?"

The man sighed. "Kid, how long did they give you?"

A low hum teased its way into Tim's hearing. "What?"

"The doctors. Your cancer doctors. How long did they give you?"

Tim sank into the leather. His fingertips tingled. "Six months. Tops."

The hum grew louder, and Tim's eyelids started to droop.

"The ship's going down, kid," Manny said gently, his voice very distant. Tim closed his eyes, and felt his arms, then his legs, detach and float away. Manny's voice was faint and followed Tim as he slipped away into nothingness. "The lifeboat's here."

The room was dark when Tim opened his eyes again. He blinked a few times then ran his tongue over the roof of his mouth. It tasted like plastic.

"Welcome back, kid."

Tim turned on his side. He was lying on a cot fitted with white sheets.

The shopkeeper was sitting next to him, leaning back in his chair, a fresh cigar clamped between his teeth. He grinned. "Sleep well?"

"Yeah," Tim muttered, then frowned. He cleared his throat. "What...." He cleared his throat again. He leaned over and spat a long string of thick, clear fluid onto the floor. "What happened?" He frowned again and shook his head.

The man leaned forward. "What's your name, kid?"

Tim passed a hand over his forehead. "I... I'm... Tim. I'm Tim."

The man laughed gruffly. "Give the kid a gold star."

Tim frowned. "My voice…"

"That's the first thing that throws everybody. Don't worry. You'll get used to it."

"Throws…" Tim stammered.

Then it all came back in a rush.

Tim sat up quickly.

"Hey, careful there, kid, you don't want to damage the syntho so soon."

Tim held his arms out in front of him. Strong arms. Smooth skin. He reached up and felt his chin, his cheeks, the stubble rasping as his fingertips ran along it. He felt his chest and noticed that he was wearing the green tank top he came in with. He gazed at it for a moment, amazed at how different it looked now that it was on a chest with definition. He blinked and looked around the room.

His body lay limp on the dentist's chair.

Tim felt faint. "Oh, God."

He swung his legs over the side of the cot, tried to stand, and immediately slumped.

The shopkeeper was at his side, holding his elbow. "Easy there, kid. The chip is still syncing up with this body's nervous system."

Tim leaned against the man and felt a strange shiver of electricity run through his arms and legs, then fade. He looked down at his feet and took a small, shuffling step. Then another. He raised his head and walked, careful but steady, to his body. It lay there, naked and limp, the eyes half closed and cloudy, the lips beginning to slip back from the teeth.

"I'm dead," Tim breathed.

"No," Manny said. "That's not you anymore."

Tim nodded, but couldn't take his eyes off those teeth, those sad precursors of bone exposed to any watching eyes.

"What do I do with it?" he murmured.

He saw the shopkeeper shrug out of the corner of his eye. "Your choice, kid. It's not syntho, so it will start to rot." Tim recoiled, and the man snorted. "I'm just saying, kid. You need to dispose of it."

"So what do I do?"

"Well," Manny said as he took Tim's arm and guided him away from the body. "You can take it to a disposal service. Or," he spread his hands, "you could pay me an extra hundred or so… and I'll take care of it for ya."

Tim turned his head and eyed Manny. "I take it that's a good deal?"

The shopkeeper grinned and clamped the cigar between his teeth again. "The best, kid."

Tim left the shop and headed toward the lights of the main drag, emerging from the darkness of the side street into the neon bustle of the city at night. He walked down the sidewalk and could feel every movement of muscle, every press of bone, every expanse of his lungs and beat of his heart. His mouth still felt sticky and tasted chemical, and he ran his tongue over his teeth, noticing how even the shape was foreign.

He saw a drug store and stopped in to buy a soda. When he emerged again he popped open the can and took a sip. His throat rippled, pushing the liquid down, a sensation so strange that he gagged. He waited for a moment, then took another sip, with the same result. The third sip he managed without gagging. He leaned against the wall and watched the passersby as he drank the rest of the soda, doing his best to ignore the oddity of his swallowing mechanism. He saw many copies of the hot actor from the most recent blockbuster, and a few copies of the latest supermodel to grace the cover of fashion magazines. They appeared natural at a cursory glance, but if he looked close, he could see how the neon reflected dully off the synthetic skin. He looked at his own arms and smiled wryly to see the same artificial glow.

Then he saw *her*.

She was wearing a red sun dress, and the skin on her exposed arms and shoulders was smooth and soft and natural. She was an original. As she passed, Tim could smell her perfume, a tantalizing play of honeysuckle and jasmine. His heartbeat quickened; his breath became shallow.

There was a crunching noise. Tim looked down. His hand had crushed the soda can.

There was no time to worry about that.

He dropped the can and followed her.

He walked behind her and watched how she moved, her skirt swishing back and forth with each step. His hands curled and uncurled. His eyes narrowed. He wanted to touch her, to taste her.

A small voice in his head asked why he was doing this. His heart paid no heed and kept racing. "It's wrong," he whispered. "It's wrong." But his fingers kept curling and uncurling. The voice told him to stop. His feet ignored and kept walking.

When the woman in the red dress turned into an alley, he followed. When the sound of the street had faded to a dull murmur behind them, he grabbed her. In the dark of the alley, in the sweet sour scent of the nearby dumpster, against the rough brick wall, his fingers sank into the flesh of her neck. She fought him, and she was strong, but he was stronger. He lowered her to the ground as her struggles weakened and watched the life seep out of her eyes.

Done. It was done.

He stood over the body, looking down at his shaking hands.

"What did I do?" he whispered. "What the hell did I do?"

Sirens wailed to life in the distance, and he looked up, eyes wide. He did the only thing he could think of, the only thing that mind and body would both assent to.

He ran.

About the Author

Eileen Maksym is the author of *Haunted,* a YA paranormal novella about a trio of ghost hunters. Her short fiction has appeared in *The Nth Degree* and *5×5*. Eileen studied philosophy at Yale and theology at Boston College and now uses both to write science fiction. She has worked in a museum in Salem, MA, in a Jesuit seminary, and in a Chicago funeral home. Currently she is an academic nomad, following her astrophysicist husband around the world, two kids in tow. When not writing or kid wrangling, Eileen is a hopeless fangirl, and can be found on Twitter (@eileenmaksym) squealing over her favorite shows, most of which involve famous detectives, dashing time travelers, and creatures that are never, ever referred to as zombies.

Website: eileenmaksym.com

E-mail: eileen.maksym@gmail.com

THIRD WORLD
Gregory L. Norris

The gonging, far away cadence drew closer. Binda attempted to put distance between her and it, only the klaxon grew louder until it stood beside her, screaming in her ear. All alarm bells were malevolent. This one didn't belong to the Overlocker at work or to any of the manufacturing machines in her quad at the factory, signaling that needles had stitched through flesh, likely bone, too. Losing a finger was bad enough; two or a limb condemned the unfortunate victim to more than the initial lightning strike of pain. Addiction to whatever meds the injured managed to score on the streets after being cut loose from the Brand's compensation, which only ran a paltry sum of weeks. A life of begging for alms after losing living unit privileges. And a short one, hungry and miserable.

This alarm sounded hungry, too like the heavy-duty machines in Binda's workroom. Thirsty, for blood. And something more. Deeper. What the Brand sometimes called a 'soul' when its supervisors preached to the workers to increase productivity. So thirsty, so near—

Binda jolted awake. The klaxon stabilized, and she quickly identified it. She was right about its thirst for blood, its hunger for tendons and skin. It was the duty alarm, screaming at her to wake up. Screaming that she was dangerously close to being late for her next shift.

The staircase had bottled the morning's already miserable heat, magnifying the odors of sweat and refuse within the too-tight press of the walls. Breathing through her mouth, Binda again imagined herself spiraling down the levels the way she had sometimes seen water circle around a drain in sections of the quad that boasted indoor plumbing.

Another colorless morning waited outside, oppressively damp from the humidity. The platinum disk of the sun floated behind the banks of smog, like a giant, unblinking eye focused solely upon her. Binda had never missed a shift, and didn't plan to on this day. She hopped on the 6:30 transport, only the second time she'd taken the Third & Last.

The transport cut through the gray landscape of the Walled City. Binda sat with her head lowered and her tired eyes aimed at the floor which was muddy from the treads of previous passengers. She did her best to not gaze out the grimy windows. The long ranges made from the living quarters for factory workers blotted out most of anything worth seeing, except at the break near the Administration Center, where a thin wedge of open ground flashed views of the spaceport. In recent days—how many, she couldn't tell, because the days had blurred together, one no different than its predecessor or that which followed—she'd noticed Brand Security visible on the streets, while palmists weren't.

An ugly, inelegant vessel sat parked on the tarmac, belching oily smoke from various vents. Not a cargo transport, no, this arrival to the Walled City was smaller, more officious-looking. An inspection, likely. That explained the absence of beggars.

Binda forgot to blink and turn her eyes away, back down in the direction of the Third & Last's dirty floor. A man in a crisp blue Brand Security uniform was attacking what looked to be a pile of dirty rags against the side of the next residential building. Binda saw the spark from his stun stick, and then a face in pain jutting up from the rags, a face that looked decades older than her nine years but couldn't have been because almists on the streets of the Walled City never lasted that long.

The terrible vision was there one second and gone the next in the time between blinks. The transport chugged onward, its angry grunts sending vibrations up through the polymer floor and into Binda's aching bones.

She passed through the main gate on foot and trudged into the long lines, clutching at her I.D. wristband. Without the band, she would be denied access to the factory. For a while now, Binda had developed a fixation on holding the device in her clutches out of fear that someone would steal it. Foolish, she knew. Who would willingly condemn themselves to this miserable place? Still, she held it tightly; it was all that kept her from living with the almists.

Binda shuffled forward. The throngs tightened into columns, single file. She thought of veins filled with corpuscles, narrowing into capillaries. The blood of the Brand. Exhaustion again threatened to overwhelm her. The odor of her fellow workers choked in her nostrils—unwashed hair and skin, sweat, breath. She thought for the hundredth time about inhaling through her mouth, only to do so would mean tasting the fetor as well as smelling it. She attempted to focus; only ten hours and she would be back on her cot, sleeping. Sleep was good. Sleep was holy. She only needed to get through the day, and then her reward would be waiting. And when she slept, her mind was free to wander to the buffet halls of the Brand's noblest supervisors, where roasted meats and slices of fruit and confections littered tabletops, stacked dozens deep atop sterling platters. Or to cool, grassy realms where she could rest her tired head, free from all burdens.

Binda blinked and moved forward. Another dozen workers to get through the turnstile, followed by a brisk march through the long network of corridors leading to a longer work shift. She gripped her wristband, held it aloft when she reached the front of the line, and waited for the scanner to grant permission to enter.

The Overlocker stitched.

Binda fed cloth into the machine's sharp teeth, her tiny hands avoiding their bite. She sensed the monster's eyes upon her, eight red sensors, round and glowing, designed for quality control and efficiency. A spider's eyes, she sometimes thought, usually when bedraggled. Wolf spiders flourished in the Walled City, some growing bigger than the size of her hands. Worse, she sensed the Overlocker's thirst for blood.

Stay focused, she told herself. One slip up could cost a finger. Or two. She slid the heavy material into the machine's maw, and the spider stitched.

During mid-meal rations, while Binda snacked on gel lets, Exalted Supervisor Emile called the quad to attention. She choked down the last of the allotment. Though hungry, the mix of liquid and protein solids went down with difficulty and complained in Binda's gut.

"It is with great pride that I announce to you a new initiative from our glorious Brand nobility at Corporate Center," the three-dimensional projection boomed. "Word of escalating conflict between the Bellerophon Procure and Atchity Stratagem. The need for Brand services has now expanded to profit beyond belief. As such—"

Supervisor Emile's smile widened, and the air took on a cool, miraculous fragrance—a smell of something green but also sweet, unlike the poisonous ivies that flourished in alleys and the abandoned spaces in the Walled City, along with the wolf spiders. *Flowers?* Binda knew the word, though her mind struggled to form an exact image. Cool, scented air rained down from the vents.

"—mandatory overtime for all workers. Blessed be the Brand!"

Numerous mouths moved around her, repeating the supervisor's words. But to Binda's ear, the hymn sounded more like the dirges she sometimes heard when almists held curbside services for their deceased.

More work. There was never less, only more.

The mandatory overtime stretched four and a half hours past her usual shift. A new pattern and different fabrics entered the quad—bolts of severe black from which stiff trousers and tunics emerged to match the military boots being churned out en masse at the neighboring quad's assembly. An insignia got added past the long rows of spider-monster Overlockers, that of a human form riding a winged animal Binda knew was a horse. She'd never seen a real one, but had ridden a horse made of wood that rocked in the long-gone world of girlhood.

Uniforms for the Bellerophon Procure's side of the new war that would, she assumed, keep her late at the quad through an unknown number of nights. Elsewhere in some different quad, perhaps in another Walled City, Brand workers were manufacturing styles for the combatants on the other side, the Atchity Stratagem's foot soldiers.

More work would mean more Vit-coin. Not enough to buy her way out of the Walled City or away from the factories. Her thoughts drifted to the spacecraft parked on the tarmac she'd spied during a morning ride that now seemed days, not hours, in the past. A supervisor here for inspection, of course. Especially with a new war brewing, and new need for the Brand's factories. There'd be a buffet on board that ship, or one laid out in the palace beyond the city's walls, which was sometimes partly visible when the smog blew away at the right angles. A palace with walls of yellow stone, its steeples pointing up, up. If she saved enough Vit-coin and honored her work, she might buy a place among the blue uniforms. And from there—

Pain slammed into Binda. She froze and bit back the urge to cry out, to *scream*. The time-delay passed; the jolt rushed up Binda's arm. The Overlocker's needle ripped free from her left pointer finger, stealing a chunk of flesh in the process. She only hoped no bone had been sacrificed to feed its hunger. As the horror sank in, she removed her hands from the maw. The machine's eight spider eyes tracked her movements, and the stitching of black cloth into uniforms ground to a halt.

Motion teased the corner of Binda's eye—blue, the slither of a floor supervisor wandering closer, alerted to the halt of industry.

"Worker?" a voice asked.

Binda flexed her bleeding finger and inserted her hands back into the maw. The monster resumed chewing on material, along with more of her blood, now secretly spilling into the black cloth.

"My apologies, Supervisor," she said.

She willed the tears from her eyes and masked her pain with a blank expression. The supervisor exhaled through nostrils and continued past Binda's workstation. A nick, that's all it was. Not her first, likely not her last. She'd gotten lazy and distracted. She was so tired, so desperate for rest. All the Vit-coins in the universe no longer mattered.

She'd gotten lucky. The needle had only grazed her finger and was so hot at the time after hours of nonstop motion that it had also cauterized the bleeding.

Before hopping on the Over-the-Moon Transport, she paid for a steri-bandage from the nearest first aid kit and wound it over the wound, hoping she hadn't waited too long. An infection, she knew, could be worse than the original injury. She winced. Her entire hand felt part of the accident. All of her aches attempted to link up on the ride back through the Walled City's deserted streets. Binda dragged herself up the steps, one level to the next. Sleep claimed her seconds after she collapsed onto her cot.

She plunged past dreams into a state of consciousness on a deeper level, one devoid of all visions.

A far away gonging sounded in the darkness. It drew closer. Binda's wounded finger pulsed between the beats. The exquisite pain shocked her awake. She recognized the noise for what it was and sat up. Another morning, a new work shift to get through. Her injured finger had thickened around the burn. She could barely flex it as she reached for her wrist I.D. on her way out the door.

About the Author

Writer Gregory L. Norris grew up on a healthy dose of creature double features and classic science fiction TV. A former feature writer and columnist at SCI FI, the official magazine of the Sci Fi Channel (before all those ridiculous Ys invaded), Norris once worked as a screenwriter on two episodes of Paramount's STAR TREK: VOYAGER series. He is the author of the handbook to all-things-Sunnydale, THE Q GUIDE TO BUFFY THE VAMPIRE SLAYER, and two paranormal romance novels offered as part of Home Shopping Network's "Escape With Romance" line—the first time HSN has offered novels to their global customers. Norris judged the 2012 Lambda Awards for excellence in GLBT writing in the SF/F/H category. In 2014, Norris was hired as screenwriter on two feature films, including the terrifying horror movie, BRUTAL COLORS (releasing in first quarter 2015). Twice, his short stories have notched Honorable Mentions in Ellen Datlow's YEAR'S BEST anthologies. Recent short story appearances include WICKED SEASONS, ANTHOLOGY YEAR III (the companion book to Anthocon, an annual conference for genre writers and readers), and ENTER AT YOUR OWN RISK: DREAMSCAPES INTO

DARKNESS, which also features reprints by Mary Shelley, Sir Arthur Conan Doyle, and Edgar Allen Poe. Norris lives in and writes from the mountains of New Hampshire, in a beautiful old New Englander house called Xanadu. His career has been featured numerous times in print interviews, on radio, and on television.

http://www.gregorylnorris.blogspot.com/

Survival
Brant Peery

I duck under a fallen street lamp and dodge into a side alley. It is dark and smells like a combination of rotting metal, mossy mud, and sewage. It is the smell of the people who have already given up and now simply exist because they haven't died yet. I recognize the blank look on their faces. Mine had once looked like that.

Survival. The word burns in my mind. I will never give up again; I have to keep moving. My legs ache—I am so tired. The climb down to the under-city has torn little holes in the legs of my cargo pants. I have to find somewhere to hide—and sleep, if I can. I feel the accumulated grime from this place on my face. My fine brown hair, now matted to near black, is crusted and stuck to my forehead with a mixture of mud, filth, and humidity. I feel so disgusting, but at least here I can buy myself some time to think things through a little.

I had been lied to; that much is clear, even in early memories of the island. What I didn't expect is that everyone else had also been lied to. I had to find out why. Why is my family dead? Why is this world mostly destroyed? I had to know the truth because what the government tells the people is just lies. With the truth, perhaps I can find a way off this trash-hole of a planet.

For now, though, I have to sleep, then find food. I feel my body forcing me to slow down. It is amazing now what I can do, but I am not completely in control anymore. I have to sleep to pacify what is in me. I find a spot to sit. Resting my back against the slick wall, I slide down to a squat, hug my knees against my chest, and rest my head against them. I let my eyes close, knowing the nightmares that await me in my mind. I try to push happier thoughts to my subconscious so they will take over while I sleep. It doesn't work. It never does. Darkness overtakes me.

"Jenny," I heard my mom saying. "You really need to get back to the piano. You promised your dad you would practice if he imported it."

I had actually wanted the stupid thing when I cried and begged my dad to spend the money to have a real piano imported from Earth. He had agreed only when I promised to actually learn to play it. He told me that it would be good to learn a muscle skill that couldn't be simply uploaded. The piano came with the download that instantly taught me all the theory, but come to find out, the download couldn't make my fingers play. I didn't understand how hard it would be when I begged for it, and now they forced me to practice so that I could "learn" it. I huffed, but sat down to play. This was so unfair.

I was distracted by thoughts of school. Jeremiah had asked stupid Amy to the dance. I hated her. She thought she was *all that* just because she could hit a stupid ball. I was never coordinated enough for sports. I was good at flirting, though. And I had already developed good-sized boobs. I fit the perfect mold of what a girl should be. I was thin with a clear, soft complexion. I dressed trendy and wore expensive clothes and makeup. I didn't understand why he didn't like me. I had even let it slip that I could play the piano when we were talking during lunch. He once told me he loved the piano, the real piano, the kind you can only find on earth. The kind that were way too expensive for anyone, especially Amy's family, to afford to import to this planet. I had wanted to learn to play just for him. But now he was with someone else. My heart ached while I practiced the runs with my fingers and imagined ways to embarrass Amy.

The memory-dream starts to fade. I don't remember much of my life before the Island. Dreams help me to piece my fragmented memories together. This dream helps me to remember my life just before the outbreak. I remember this day with equal bits of bitterness and fondness. It had been a time in my life when I was safe, with my parents. Life made sense back then. In the darkness between dreams, I still feel the disappointment of lost love as a 14-year-old. Looking back now, I regret being so spoiled. Back then I only saw my life as a way to get things. My dad was rich, well, very rich, and I wanted everything that he had that would make me popular. I almost cry. I can't remember much about him except that he loved me so much more than I deserved. I remember him singing to me at night to calm me when I was afraid of the dark. But try as hard as I can, I can't remember his face. Even in my dreams, he is always either obscured or turned away from me. In my heart, I miss him, but I barely remember him. Even though I have perfect recollection of everything I see both in and out of dreams, there is very little of it that actually makes sense. It is hard to put everything in order when there is really no base to start from.

The dreams I have these days are not like normal people's dreams. I don't process random stuff at night in an unconscious jumble of disconnected non-realities. I am fully aware of this dream, which is in fact a memory, down to the last detail. I will remember this dream down to the last perfect detail when I wake too. It is like having an eidetic memory, but it is delivered to me as random parts of my life. Sometimes I am a baby remembering my first moments of life. That is a weird experience, by the way. Sometimes it is after the plague, and I am remembering the isolation districts and Island hospitals. The order never makes sense. I am being played back my life in random. It helps me to fill in my memory, which is mostly nonexistent or fuzzy. I figure that must be a side effect of dying.

The blackness of between the dreams starts to fade, and a hospital room starts to materialize. I recognize this room immediately and scream in despair. I am at my mother's bedside. She is looking at me.

"NO! I DON'T WANT TO SEE THIS!!" I panic. I try to force the dream to change. "No…" I cry. But the memory continues. I scream as I am absorbed completely by the dream.

She looked at me. She was so beautiful, even though her eyes were sunk in and much of her hair had now fallen out. People used to tell me that I looked like her. When she was well, she had been thin and strong and above all, beautiful. Lying on the bed, she still looked regal to me, even though she was terminally ill with the virus. She stared at me, and in her she feebleness tried to sit up, but could only muster a head raise. I was crying.

I knew I wasn't supposed to be in here. I was kneeling at her bedside because I had run away from my caretakers and sneaked into the hospital no one wanted to be in. I didn't care anymore, though. Dad had died from this same virus, and I didn't even get to say goodbye or anything. They had burned him right after as they did everyone who died here. Mom was all I had left, and I didn't want to live anymore if she died, too. So here I was, looking into her eyes, amazed at the paleness of her skin and her sunken cheeks.

"Take me with you," I pleaded as she looked at me. Surprise crossed her face as she finally recognized me.

"No, Gennevieve, it can't be you." Her face contorted with the pain of knowing I was here. "We took such great care to ensure you would leave this forsaken planet."

The words, accompanied by her horrified look, made me realize that I had hurt her now more than anyone else ever had.

"You obstinate child, all that planning… You will get it too, and… and…" she couldn't finish. "Your dad always said you were strong and clever, but that does you no good if you act stupidly!" she chided. This was a lecture I had heard before. This time, however, I think I understood it, one stupid act too late, it would seem. The anger quickly left her face and was replaced by what seemed to be regret. She couldn't even cry as her body didn't have enough strength to make tears. She sobbed silently, though, the anguish evident in her eyes. I had never seen her so upset, not even on the day the doctors told her dad had died. She knew, just like me, that I would now die of the same thing that was ravaging her. The thing that had killed dad, and almost two-thirds of the population of our planet.

At that moment, looking into the despair of my

mother's face, I felt a regret far stronger than anything I had felt before. I should have gone off the planet as my parents had planned. When I ran away, I had only been thinking of myself and how I didn't want to be alone. I had only felt the pain of losing them both and how that had been so unfair. I wanted to die, too, and this seemed like the most poetic way to go, just like them. But now, looking into my mother's eyes as she stared at me, I knew I had made a mistake. She so desperately wanted me to live, and now, just like everyone else who got this virus, I would die.

I took her hand as tears streamed down my face. I looked into her eyes. They softened, and she smiled. "It is good to see you one last time." She coughed. Blood spattered the bed sheets. Pain shot across her face, but she quickly hid it.

"Promise me you will survive." She looked at me so intensely. "It has been done, you can beat it. Your father..." cough, "promise me," cough, cough, "... promise me," she insisted through her coughing fit.

I couldn't help it. I knew that no one survives once they catch the virus. But I opened my mouth to promise any-way. "Mom," I said through tears, "I promi—"

Her eyes rolled back into her head and she started to convulse. Her body shook violently.

"Mom! Mommy! I promise, Mom! I promise! Just

don't leave me!" I half-yelled, half-sobbed. I looked around. "Someone help!" I knew no one would come. This is where they put the ones who won't make it, the ones that the virus had already killed. Here is where they put them so they could die and be burned.

"Mommy!" I yelled and shook her. She stiffened suddenly and exhaling, went limp. I watched as the light left her eyes. My anchor in everything in my life now lay dead in front of me. I hugged her body and sobbed into her gown. Her life had been stolen by the very virus I caught when I walked into this room. I wanted to die with her now. But knowing that her last wish was for me to survive, I knew now I had to find a way.

I heard the flat-line of the computer's long, mourning beep to announce the virus had claimed another life. Looking at the screen, I could see an incinerator countdown had started. I jolted to the door, knocking down a tray as I ran. I pulled on the door to escape before the computer turned on the gas. I heard the igniters clicking.

The door wouldn't budge. It was already auto locked. I desperately pulled, put my foot on the door frame and pulled and jerked at the handle. It didn't give. I could hear a roar like a dragon's breath in the room. I could feel the heat as a dozen jets of flame lit up the room.

I desperately pounded on the glass of the door, crying out for help as I saw a dark skinned nurse walk by.

He stopped and looked in at me and just shook his head. I could feel my clothes catch on fire, my shoes melting off my feet. My jacket burned up my back. I regretted that for just a moment – I really liked that jacket. But, as soon as my hair caught on fire, the jacket was quickly forgotten.

My body was pure pain, the skin on my legs burning first as the rest of me caught. I screamed and spun, tripping onto my mother's bed. Just before the pain-induced blackness took me, I looked into her open eyes and apologized for not fulfilling her last wish. At least I would die here with her.

I jolt awake, screaming. Instantly, the smell of filth offending my nose reminds me that I am still in the under-city. Physical pain doesn't bother me much anymore, but that… I had tried so hard to forget that hospital room. Now I will see it in perfect detail forever.

Still slightly dazed, I look up. A group of men hanging around a burn barrel in the distance are now staring at me. My scream must have drawn their attention. Damn, I had wanted to go unnoticed. I lower my head and will them to look away, but I can tell by the hungry, toothless smiles growing on their faces that they plan on instituting their version of the declared 'martial law', which down here means the biggest, meanest group rules. They will invite me to join them, they will offer their protection, but really it is just to be their whore. At least until they get bored with me or really drunk, then they will trade or kill me.

Of course, I will refuse. Any self respecting 16-year-old girl would. Then they will teach me why I need their protection. It isn't a good situation for most lone girls. Unfortunately for them, I am not like most 16-year-old girls.

They start towards me, walking in a formation of leader and two wingmen on each side. Likely, they will try to surround me. I get flashbacks of the Island. I hate guys like this. Not even worthy to be called animals. Looking past them, I see a girl hiding in the corner, watching them as they approach me. Probably one of the girls they "protect". She looks like she wants to run. Something is making her stay.

She stands as the group moves past her. "Why don't you leave this one alone?" she says in a flirtatious voice. "Come, take me instead. I already know how you like it."

"Sit down and shut up, you cow," the leader says.

"You will get your turn later," one of the others say as they pass her.

She doesn't sit, she just stares at them. She looks over at me as if to say "run", but we both know that with dogs, running just makes it worse. I feel the bile start to build in my throat. I know I am going to have to kill to get out of this. I hate killing, even scum like this who deserve it. I hate the way it makes me feel afterward. I remember the training sessions on the Island. I was never as strong as they wanted me to be on the Island. I would often choose to be killed instead of to kill.

People shouldn't have to kill to survive. I could choose death now. Avoid the darkness of the abyss that comes with taking a life. I look up again at the group moving towards me. I can't let them kill me. In the state between dead and healing, the Island will find me. Anger rises in me as I watch the scum men approach. It is their fault I have to live like this. I hate them and all who are like them for turning this world into a cesspool of constant pain.

As they get closer, their stench nearly numbs my nose and causes my eyes to tear up. Sweat mixed with shit and garbage. Most of their teeth are missing in front. Probably from fighting. It really is a hard life down here, and these guys make it harder. I begin to stand, consciously taking a weak stance by shrugging my shoulders forward and staying low enough I have to look up at them.

The one that must be their leader begins to speak to me. Boy, he is ugly. Kind of scrawny and has a gut that would make a swine proud. His hair is long and matted down. As he smiles at me, I notice he is missing more than a few teeth. They probably abandoned their post gladly, fleeing his mouth in joy just to get away from his horrible breath.

"I haven't seen you around here before. Let me explain the rules to you a bit, as they differ here in my part of town," Stinky Breath says as he spreads his arms out and turns, as if to look upon his kingdom. "Here, not everyone is as generous and kind as I am." His posse snickers at that. "I am someone who can protect you from those who would take advantage of your youth and beauty." He reaches out to touch my hair, and I back away. He smiles. "What do you say? Will you accept my protection and join us?"

He and his posse surround me, moving closer. They are all close enough now to grab me. Their trap is fully set. He grins his hideous smile, surely thinking of me with my clothes ripped and me being held down first for him, then the others, regardless of my answer. They probably don't get many young girls anymore as most of them would have already joined a gang. This must feel like a special treat. He waits for me to respond, already lost in his fantasy.

"No," I respond, "as appealing as your offer is, I must decline. I will let you live, though, if you run now and leave her behind." I point at the woman who tried to distract them. They laugh. As much as I hate guys like this, I want to give them a chance to live. Life is hard, and they are just a product of that. "Please go, I don't want this."

"You hear that boys!" he says between chuckles. "She doesn't want this, and she is going to let us live! She is right about both those things. She won't want what is coming, and compared to that old whore behind us, having this feisty little girl is going to make us feel more alive than we have in weeks!" They are all laughing at his humorous twists of my words. I guess they have decided.

With my back several feet from the wall, I stand to my full height, easily taller than any of them by a few inches. My back straightens and my legs tense in preparation; I can feel power grow in me as a virus-enhanced adrenaline starts to flood my body. I see the surprise in his eyes. *I bet you didn't see this coming, asshole*, I think as I leap forward with more power and quickness than should have been possible from my thin frame. The lackeys haven't caught on to what is about to happen yet.

He tries to command them to grab me quickly, but my fist is already buried in his throat, crushing his larynx, the force of my movement pushing him backwards as he trips to the ground. He grabs his crushed windpipe. He tries to scream but the only sound that comes out is a bloody gurgle. The others are slow to react. I see their fantasies melt away into terror and anger as they watch their leader dying at my feet. Some start to turn to run, but two of them move in on me.

I pity them. I hate them. I pity them for their weakness, I hate them for their inhumanity, but most of all I hate them for the pain they have purposely caused others. I recover my weight and balance quickly. Jumping slightly, I stomp hard with all my enhanced strength on the outstretched leg of the closest monster. I hear a loud pop as his leg breaks and his knee dislocates. He screams as he loses his balance, and his momentum causes him to fall past me. I feel the other man reaching for me, and as I dodge his grab for my hair, I grab Broken Knee by the jacket and pull him into my center of balance. I move with him, and like a dance, I redirect the force of my movement and his, and I throw him directly into the other man. They both crash hard to the floor.

My balance fully regained, I stomp and grind the heal of my left foot into the face on one of the heads poking out of the bastard pile on the ground. I hear a satisfying crunch as his cheekbone gives in. He stops moving. I see a knife that has fallen out of one of their hands. I pick it up, and barely aiming, throw it forcefully at one of the assholes running away. It sticks below the left shoulder blade. The man, thrown off balance, stumbles to the ground with a thud. The other guy has dodged around a corner, and by the sound of his footsteps, is running as fast as he can. I hate him, but not enough to chase him down.

Looking over the mess, I see the girl stand up next to the barrel. Now that I take the time to observe her, she is plainly one of their play toys. Abuse is evident by the open wounds on her hands and cheeks, and the bruises all over her mostly naked body. I walk over to the man who tried to run. He has sat up against a pillar, and spitting up his own blood, yells obscenities at me. A roundhouse kick to the face shuts him up. I pull the knife from his slumped back to let the blood run into his punctured lung. I wipe the blade on his coat, leaving him hacking and coughing his last breaths. I walk over to the girl.

I am surprised by her bravery as she stands her ground as I approach. The torn rags on her show the many scars that run down her thin but strong body. It looks like they had to use force every time with this one. She raises her shoulders and stands taller as I approach.

"I always thought it would be them who killed me," she says, as she looks at the heap of men by the wall. She looks back at the knife, then directly into my eyes. "At least this will be quick, I assume?"

"I am not going to kill you," I respond. "I would like you to clean up for me. I think one of them is still breathing." I hold the knife out, offering it to her.

She looks at the knife, staring at it, then at me. "What has happened to you to make you so…" She struggles for the right word. "I mean you are so… young." She hesitates, probably afraid to upset me, as she eyes the knife in my hand again and looks over at the one who tried to run. "I saw such hate in your eyes."

"Everyone has suffered the last few years," I say, looking at her scars again. "Some scars are not as visible as others."

"They killed my daughter," she whispers almost to herself as she looks down. I see the hate and pain in her eyes too.

I offer the knife again, holding it out. She looks at it, hesitating for a moment, and a fire lights in her eyes. She becomes the predator, the avenging angel. Whatever was holding her back is gone. She will never be prey again.

In silence, she walks toward the wall. Whimpering in pain, Broken Knee tries to free himself from the man on top of him. His panicked look as he watches her approach is testament to the unforgivable things he must have done to her.

"No, Nela!" he pleads. "We protected you!" Desperately, he tries to lift himself off the floor. Fingers spread wide, he reaches for her. His leg still trapped, his hand grabs her bare leg about the same time the knife finds purchase in his eye socket.

Nela drops the knife, and the head it is attached to falls to the floor with it. She stares at it for a second like she is going to lose it and run. Her expression hardens even more, and she kicks the knife further into the skull and spits on the pile.

"One of them got away," she says with force.

"Sounds like a good hunt to me," I throw over my shoulder as I am walking away in the opposite direction. I almost feel sorry for the scumbags who owe her a debt, but nah, not really.

I walk down the under-passage towards an opening in the tunnel. I hurry to get away from the scene and Nela—as

I feel my hate turning to disgust toward myself. The air is fresher here, but I feel unclean in a way the fresh air can't fix. I can taste it in my mouth now that the adrenaline is starting to wear off, and I have to suppress the crying that is starting. Tears flow down my dirty cheeks. I hate how horrible of a person I am. Add three more souls to the list of lives ended by Jen the Destroyer, cursed with the ability to survive, even though I hate what it turns me into. I feel weakness for my shame.

I am starting to shake uncontrollably. The voices of the Island trainers flood my mind with reprimand as I remember them telling me that everyone dies and that I must learn to take life to preserve life. Even now, as I consider Nela, the darkness of death pulls at my soul, and I feel that I am slipping into a deep, dark, oily pit. For what seems like the thousandth time, I consider just giving in to the monster inside. Becoming emotionally dead like the others, I saw on the Island, able to kill without regret. I am a monster, one who can't die.

The Island said we were created by God to purge the known worlds of pain and suffering and to create a utopia where no one suffers, where all are equal; a place where everyone either works for the greater good or is removed from it.

It just never sounded right to me. People should be rewarded for how they live and sacrifice. They should have the opportunity to be good, not forced. Choice is what makes us human. What do I know, though, perhaps people need that kind of order. In a world where everyone is equal, Nela's daughter might be still be with her mom.

I crouch down against a wall to regain control of myself. I miss my parents so much right now. I need Mom to tell me it is going to be okay, that I am not evil, that I only did what I had to. I hug my legs and rock myself as I picture her holding me. The sobbing slows and the shaking stops.

A notification from my bio implant wakes me from my daydream, and the message it contains shocks me back to reality. I jolt up and look around, surveying the area. I see a promising bridge in the distance and I run.

One of the watcher programs that I had installed on the police frequency had picked up *them* using my code name. I start to review the communication. It sounds like they had a call-in for the bounty from someone in the district. Probably the one who got away. I didn't think my bounty would be known down here, but if my bounty has risen high enough, every criminal of any decent amount of power would be hunting me simply for the payout. He must have put two and two together as his mind raced to figure out what had just happened to his crew. Idiot. If he had been intelligent, he would have stayed as far away from me as possible. I can't imagine the government will let anyone live if they know what I can really do. Now I really hope Nela catches up to him. Her reward to him will be quicker than the one that awaits him from the police.

I start scanning all the encrypted channels, trying to find the one that the Special Force is using. I have to find out what they know and what assets they have brought with them. I finally find the channel they are on. I pick up 3 drones and an agent. Backup is on the way.

Over the police channel, I hear "Jen…" It's him, over the police frequency, the smug little agent who lost me in the upper-city. He must have figured out I am listening in on their private little conversations. Judging by the police force and drone assets he brought with him, he is being a little more cautious this time. Must have learned his lesson last time.

"You think that you are so smart coming down here. Down here will just get you killed. Give up, let me take you back home." He could feign innocence so well. I know what *home* is like, and I will never go back there. "We only want to keep you and all these people safe."

As if to oblige, I stop running. I have reached the bridge that goes over this part of the city. In the past, this would have been busy carrying people and goods to other parts of the city in a clean and out-of-the-way fashion, as it weaved between skyscrapers 40 feet above the street. I remember riding it with my mom when she told me my dad built it. We were on the way to see my dad give a speech about the success of the colony. I look up and I can see the underside of the tracks hidden by the side supports. The track doesn't look like it has been used in a while. They must have stopped running the trains here after the outbreak.

I need to get up there. I feel power build in my legs as I flex them, readying myself for a jump to a platform halfway up one of the bridge's legs. Leaping, I grab a cross bar with one hand, and continuing my momentum, I leap towards the top of the pillar where the rails sit. Halfway there, I hear him give the command to shoot to kill to all the drones over his drone command channel. I almost miss the top platform. What a jerk. Who would kill a 16-year-old girl just because she made him look like a fool once? Or does he know who I really am? Certainly, the Island wouldn't trust their secret to a police agent.

Since that day in the hospital with my mom, I have recovered from the worst of injuries, even death on occasion. I don't know how, but it didn't seem to surprise the doctors on the Island. The only thing that I know for certain is that I feel much stronger after I have eaten. Today, I didn't get a chance to eat. The last meal I had was yesterday sometime, of raw rat. It was enough to heal the injuries I had, but didn't leave much for running like this. The fight earlier used most of my last reserves up. I feel sluggish, but I know I have to keep going.

I hear Agent Jerkface give the command to surround the area and create a detection net. I fight through the weariness and pain that is growing in my arms and legs. I hop up and hang horizontally, pressed between the two side rail supports. I'm hanging there like I am lying on my stomach on an invisible crossbeam, with my boots pressed up against one rail and my outstretched arms pressing against the opposite side in an impossible overhang under the bridge.

I scan the ground, looking for Agent Loser. I see him. He is barking out orders. I press myself closer to the underside of the bridge. They never look up when they search. Logical mistake I guess when you are chasing a 16-year-old girl. A mistake I am going to use to my advantage.

Holding myself there in this position, a memory comes to me of me doing this same type of maneuver in a tree out in our yard when I was about ten. I had jumped and grabbed the lowest branch of the tree and started to climb. I had tried to get my legs around the branch as I climbed, thinking I could lift myself out and up. I could remember the smell of the tree pressed against my face as I tried to force the climb. I could hear the gasp of my father as he saw my hands start to slip. I saw everything now that I didn't see then, the look on their faces as I fell. I could smell the fall harvest on the wind and the odor of the old factory in town. When I rotated, I could see the grass. Now I could stop the memory there and count the grass if I wanted to. I felt the pain of my arm breaking as I hit the ground.

"… everyone go into the nearest residency for scanning. This is a matter of the state, and according to ordinance

11043.c4, we will be locking all doors." His voice over the drone loudspeakers brings me back to the current time, to this memory that I am making now. He also ordered the drones to intimidate the civilians back into their homes. The drones, still scanning, start to push the curious back.

Waiting for a drone to pass underneath, I start to move slowly, holding myself tight against both sides of the bridge. This allows me to move without hanging down. It is getting harder with each hand, each leg movement I make. This particular move I learned in the compound. It allowed me access to forbidden areas without notice. Right hand and left leg move while the left hand and right leg maintain enough pressure to keep me horizontal. Like this, I move until I am almost directly above the agent barking out the orders. With my arms and legs spread like they are, I notice a stench. Oh, I think I am going to gag. Is that me? I sniff to the side of my open armpit. Oh lord, it is me. My mom would be in such a fit if she ever smelled me like this. I hope Agent Blunder down there can't smell it.

"Broaden the search circle." He was yelling at what must have been one of the local police S.W.A.T. force leaders who was reporting that they hadn't found me yet. "Damn it, we have a confirmed sighting and the best hunting drones that credit can buy!" He sounds desperate.

Accessing my data link chip mentally, I start the pro-cess of cracking the encryption wrapped around the drone-to-drone communication channel. It is harder to get in than most networks that I have encountered, but lucky for me, this was still built on the idea that intrusion detection would result in lethal feedback to the hacker, killing or incapacitating her. It stings like hell, but doesn't kill me. I heal faster than it can hurt me. Grinding my teeth, I look for the crack in the security. There. I touch the virtual knot with my mind again, and again, I am rewarded with feedback. However, this time I don't let go, and the knot starts to unwind. Like a ball of yarn being pulled straight, the virtual knot is gone, and in its place is the communication channel of the drones.

I touch the channel once again and listen. I hear them. They are reporting all the people they encounter to each other. They use the most dull and technical language. They really are boring to listen to. They all report in on their respective areas. None of them are reporting in of this area. Of course not, Agent Smarty Pants down there doesn't need any help from drones in his area. He thinks he has it covered. I had counted on that.

My legs and arms complain about the abuse that I am putting them through. It is getting hard to hold myself up this way. I need to get him to move so I can get down safely, outside his perimeter. I touch the drone communication thread again with my mind and using the most droney monotone thoughts possible, I relay, "Positive match. Female, age 16, brown hair, blue eyes, dressed in khaki cargo pants. Black shirt. Scan results: positive DNA match." Now to send them running. "Subject out of range. Moving west 10.9765.43 degrees north, 107.7630 degrees east. Grid 12. Permission to pursue?" It was hard to not let a human thought through when doing drone speech.

"Permission granted! All drones pursue in pattern Charlie!" I hear Agent Blunder practically shout through his connection chip. Really, did the man have to shout even when thinking to drones too?! I bet he is a hard man to live with. If he is married – and I don't know how he could be, I mean, he is not exactly easy to look at – but if he were married, I could only imagine the dinner conversation, "HONEY, PASS THE MILK THIS WAY! DO IT NOW!" Jerk.

Now everyone is moving in the direction I sent them. It is about a half mile down the track. I watch as my arms continue to complain. Soon they are all out of sight. I climb down the nearest pillar and jump the last 10 feet or so. I hit the ground silently next to the pillar in the street and almost immediately am rewarded with the overpowering stench of the sewer overflow in the gutters. "Wow," I whisper to myself, "at least I don't smell as bad as that."

I turn to run in the opposite direction I had sent the agent. When I turn around, my heart sinks into my stomach. There, scanning the area, is a drone the agent had left behind on a different communication channel so I couldn't sense it. He had fallen for my trap, but I had also fallen for his. It is looking directly at me now. Once it had locked on there was no way to outrun one of these. I stand there waiting for the bullets to hit.

Nothing. It just looked at me. I took the chance and charged it. It was the only thing I could think of. I leapt into the air and hung onto it before it could dodge away. Dangling from it, I lifted my fist to smash the control panel and camera.

"Please don't hurt my drone," I hear below me in a strange accent. "It took me a long time to talk one into believing I am the person who it is assigned to. They are quite stubborn."

I looked at the voice as the drone lowered me to the ground. Standing there with an energy gun in his hand is an older boy. He looks like he is anywhere between 17-20. He is old enough to grow good facial hair, but not so old to look like a true man. He is taller than me and slender, yet toned enough to see plenty of muscle under his shirt. His skin is darker than mine, like he has a perpetual tan. His eyes are brown and his shoulder length black hair is tied back in a ponytail. And he knows how to handle the gun he is holding.

"Are you just going to stand there and wait for them to come back?" he asks in that accent.

"Oh," I finally say. With difficulty, I take my eyes off him and look back at the direction the agent had run off to. "Yeah, thanks." As much as I would like to, I can't have friends, not even ones as cute as him. So I give him one more look and dash past him. He wouldn't have been able to keep up anyway. I regret for a moment the lost chance to have human company. Those kinds of thoughts are dangerous in a world where no one can be trusted.

Once again, I run.

As I run, I try to convince myself I am better off alone. Only to my surprise, the boy runs up beside me and matches pace.

"And yes, by the way, you do smell that bad." He grins. I glare as hard as I can at him. His drone follows us.

About the Author

By day, Brant Peery is a software engineer in Idaho. By night, he is a husband and a father of five. In his spare time, he enjoys playing his tin whistle, guitar, and printing plastic things in 3D. Brant has loved writing from his earliest childhood when he won a grade school writing competition. He aspires to someday get all the crazy stories out of his mind and into print so others might have a chance to live those adventures.

Unwelcome Neighbors
Gerald Rick

Tucker stepped off the drop ship and into the fresh air of the Cincinnati, Ohio spaceport. He took in a deep breath of air before letting it out through his nostrils, savoring the feeling it left in his lungs. He took a moment to appreciate the natural gravity of earth, which was much more comfortable to him than the artificial gravity in the spaceships that he had called home for the past few years.

Tucker took a moment to look up and smile at the blue sky above him.

"Daddy!" he heard a little girl excitedly scream and looked down just in time to see a little girl running towards him.

"Abigail!" Tucker shouted as he bent down to scoop his daughter into a big bear hug. She laughed as he spun her around. "I see that my little princess has done some growing while I've been away."

Abigail nodded her head and smiled a proud smile. Then her face grew solemn for a moment before she said, "I missed you, Daddy."

Tucker smiled back at her and kissed her on the forehead. "I've missed you, too, princess, but Daddy is here to stay now."

Abigail's eyes grew wide, along with her smile. "You mean you don't have to fight the aliens no more?" she asked happily.

"Nope," Tucker replied, "we beat the aliens, baby. And that means that Daddy is home for good!"

Abigail let out an excited squeal.

"I see you've told her the good news," said a voice behind Tucker. Tucker turned around to see his wife standing behind him, smiling. Tucker walked over and scooped her into a hug along with Abigail.

"God, Olivia," said Tucker as he set Abigail back down on the ground, "I swear you get more and more beautiful each time I come home."

Olivia smiled an easy smile and wrapped her arms around Tucker's neck, drawing him into a deep and passionate kiss. When she finally broke away from him, she was still smiling, "Well, I guess this is as beautiful as you'll ever see me then, because you're not setting foot on another one of those spaceships.”

Tucker smiled back at his wife. “I wouldn’t set foot on one of those ships again even if they had a gun to my head, darling. I’m home for good.”

“Daddy’s home for good!” squealed Abigail as she twirled in circles.

Tucker bent down and scooped Abigail up in his arms once again. “Speaking of home, why don’t we head that way? I’m tired of looking at this space junk. What say you all that we head back to Kentucky?”

The flat plains of Ohio quickly turned into the rolling hills of Kentucky as Tucker sped towards their home in north-eastern Kentucky. Tucker looked at Abigail in the rear-view mirror. She was fast asleep in her car seat, her light brown curls cascading down her face, her little mouth open with drool spilling out of the side. Tucker smiled.

Then Tucker looked over at his beautiful wife in the passenger seat. Olivia was sitting there with an anxious expression on her face. Her green eyes were narrowed pensively at the dash, a few strands of her dark brown hair hanging down in her face, but she paid them no mind.

“Is everything all right, sweetheart?” asked Tucker.

“Oh, yeah,” Olivia snapped her head around to look

at him and gave him a tired smile. "Well, it's just that…" Olivia trailed off.

"It's just that what, darling?" Tucker asked, a knot of nervousness forming in the pit of his stomach.

"Well," Olivia said, "I saw on the news that they are letting some of the Greymen take refuge on Earth since we destroyed their home planets."

"I know, darling. It will be alright, though. None of them will be anywhere near us way out in the country."

"That's the thing, though," said Olivia, "they said on the news that they are planning to make refugee centers out in places that weren't as populated. They said that moving them to larger cities may cause riots and stuff like that."

Tucker let out an easy laugh, "Honey, they were probably talking about places out in the Midwest. There is plenty of land to go around out there, enough to where they could build them something and keep them out of everyone's way."

"You're probably right," sighed Olivia. "Y'know, I missed having you here. You could always draw me out of my worrying moods."

Tucker reached over and grabbed her hand. "That's what I'm here for, darling." Then he brought her hand up to his mouth and kissed it gingerly before placing it on his lap. "Now let's just hope that this nap Abigail is taking doesn't make her stay up late into the night," said Tucker playfully as he moved Olivia's arm up his leg. "I believe that we have a lot of catching up to do in some departments."

Olivia laughed and pulled her hand out of his grip. "Oh, stop it," she said, but then she winked and continued, "Contain yourself while your daughter is asleep in the back. There will be plenty of time for that tonight."

The rest of the drive passed by with Tucker and Olivia flirting like a high school couple while Abigail slept on in the back seat.

Eventually they passed a sign that said, *Welcome to Lewis County, Kentucky!* Tucker rolled down his window and took in a deep breath of the fresh Kentucky air. "Ahh, it feels good to be home."

Tucker drove by the little town of Vanceburg, Kentucky. The place had not changed a bit since he grew up here as a kid, let alone in the years since he had been in the service.

Any other time, Tucker would have driven through Vanceburg, but he was more than ready to be home. Vanceburg would always be there, as little and as quaint as ever.

Tucker drove a few more miles until the few lights of Vanceburg were out of view, and then he pulled off the highway onto a small, one-lane road that ran beside Kinniconick Creek. Before long he was pulling into a driveway leading up to a doublewide trailer.

Tucker got out of the car, opened the door to the backseat, and whispered to Abigail, "Wake up beautiful. We are home."

Tucker woke up the next morning to the sound of birds outside his window. He opened the blinds of the window and saw the sun beginning to rise over the hills that ran along either side of the holler. He heard Abigail laughing in the living room, so he slid some shorts on and got out of bed.

"Well, good morning, sleepyhead," said Olivia. She was cooking breakfast, and from the popping and sizzling coming from the pan, Tucker could guess she was making her famous bacon and eggs. He walked over towards her and gave her a kiss on the cheek.

"Good morning, angel," Tucker said, and then he added in a much lower whisper, "I wouldn't have slept so long if someone hadn't kept me up into the wee hours of the morning."

Olivia laughed, then she quietly added, "Don't act like you didn't enjoy it."

"Daddy, Daddy, look!" yelled Abigail, drawing Tucker's attention away from Olivia. "Look at the big trucks!"

"What is it, baby?" asked Tucker as he walked over beside his daughter.

"Look at the big trucks," squealed Abigail again as she pointed out the window.

Tucker followed her finger and saw the big government trucks that were parked at the end of their driveway.

"What in the world?" asked Tucker, more to himself than to Abigail or Olivia.

"Oh no," gasped Olivia, worry apparent in her voice. "What are they doing here?"

"Just stay in the house, you two, I'm sure everything is all right," Tucker reassured Olivia. "I'll go outside and see what's going on."

Tucker went back into the bedroom and tugged on a white shirt. He walked out their front door and strode up to one of the trucks. "You mind me asking what's going on here?" Tucker yelled up to one of the men driving the trucks.

"Government sanctioned part of this property to build a refugee center for the Greymen," yelled the driver over the engine.

Tucker's face instantly grew hot, "Why wasn't I told about this? This is my property!"

"Hey man, don't go gettin' all red at me. I'm just following orders. You wanna talk to the man in charge, he's on the other side of the truck scopin' out the place!"

Tucker walked over to the side of the truck the man had directed him towards and saw a man in a suit. "You mind telling me what's going on here?" asked Tucker.

"Part of your land has—"

"Yeah, yeah, been sanctioned," Tucker cut the guy off. "Listen, ain't none of those grey bastards going to come live next to me. I just got done fighting a war against those bastards, I saw them kill my friends, I saw them blow apart ships full of our people. You ain't gonna put a refugee center for them bastards right next to my damned house."

The guy in the suit stared at Tucker a moment before he said, "I don't care what you saw out there in space. I don't care how many of your friends got blown to bits—the refugee center is going here. This is where the government said to build one, so we are building one. You got a problem with it, move your ass to one of the bigger cities. The government is keeping the Greymen far away from there."

"You gotta be shittin' me," yelled Tucker. "Give me the number to your boss, I'm gonna give him a piece of—"

"A piece of what?" the man in the suit cut Tucker off as he drew his suit jacket back to reveal a badge that identified him as General Frank White.

"You think that badge gives you any respect in my eyes?" spat Tucker. "I'm out of the service as of yesterday. If that badge does anything for you in my eyes, it makes you despicable. How can you let them build this? After you saw what they tried to do to us until we drove them back, after you saw them kill your soldiers, how are you letting this happen?"

"I'm letting it happen because it has to happen," replied the General coolly. "Now please, go back inside to your family before I call the police and have you arrested for obstruction."

Tucker's eyes narrowed at the general. "You wouldn't dare."

"You just try me and see," replied the general as he pulled a hologram projector out of his pocket.

Tucker turned to walk away, but before he could round the corner of the truck, he let his anger get the best of him one last time. "This won't happen!" yelled Tucker at the general. "Not on my property! My little girl isn't going to grow up next to those monsters!"

The general simply turned and stared at Tucker, then said, "Then I suggest you pack up your family and move your ass somewhere else, because I'm building this refugee center right next to your goddamned trailer whether you like it or not."

Tucker looked at the general. He'd been in long enough to know that there would be no fighting this. He went back inside and retrieved his pistol.

About the Author

Gerald Rick is a first-time author who finally set out to tell the story that kept coming back in his mind. When he's not working in the shop getting his hands dirty, or learning everything he can about writing, he spends his time with his wife and three kids out camping.

ELYSIA

Josh Schwartzkopf

"That's the problem. We don't know how it spreads," said the old man, waving his wooden cane at the crowd. "We've tried boiling the water we drink. We've tried face-masks. We've even quarantined the sick, and yet it keeps spreading."

Murmurs filled the small space that served as the council chambers. Men, women, and children huddled on the dirt floor. Dirt the color of ash.

"It has to be manufactured. There's no other explanation," a woman pleaded, clutching a sleeping infant to her bosom.

"Let's not start this argument again," said a younger man who stood behind the hollow log. The log that served as a table for the council. "It doesn't matter if it was manufactured or not. We need to find out how it spreads and save those who are still alive."

In the back of the room, longing to return to his

home, stood a young black man with a neon orange mohawk running down his scalp and a similar patch of facial hair on his chin. His name was Randyll Dougherty, and he was only sixteen years old. Sixteen years old and he was the last surviving member of his family—at least, when his father passed he would be the last one. That is why he was selected to attend this special meeting of the colony council.

"But if we discover that it was manufactured, then perhaps we can also find the cure!" an old woman cried, waving her arms frantically in the air.

"Enough! We must have order here!" a bearded man at the center of the council table said, slamming a meaty hand into the hollow log. This was the leader of the colony, Danyeel Makkensy."Now Padres Viktor had the floor, and we will listen to what he has to say. No more interruptions."

The old man with the wooden cane cleared his throat and gazed out across the sea of tired faces. He scanned the humid room built from scraps of the starship that took them to this new planet. The same ship that was supposed to be their salvation from the dying Earth. Now all that remained was the metal hull, bent and shaped to serve as shanties for the colonists who could not afford to live in the majestic city a few miles away.

"We've tried everything but one thing…prayer," the padres said, and immediately the room erupted. Some cried out indignantly, saying that this was the preaching of a lunatic, whereas others fell to their knees, holding their hands up to the ceiling, saying that prayer was the only way out of this nightmare.

"And what should we pray for?" the young man, Randyll, bellowed, his strong and powerful voice sailing over the din of the crowd. The padres heard him and with a motion of his cane, the room went silent.

"How can you ask that, my son? You, whose father is our spiritual leader. The same man who baptized us all as Children of Gaia. We pray to the Mother. We pray that she end this punishment and restore us back into the light."

"My father prayed for all of that before my mother died," Randyll grumbled, letting his hatred pour out and cover the simpering fools who looked at him now. "She was one of the first to succumb to the Deadly Tears. And now he is dying from the same disease. No, prayer isn't going to work."

"Maybe we pray to the wrong goddess," a young woman whispered, and Randyll fixed his weary eyes on her.

"That is just a myth, there is no evidence that this person even exists," the padres interjected.

"How do we know that Gaia exists either, Padres?" Randyll scoffed, shaking his head as he ran a trembling hand through his orange hair."I can't listen to this bullshit anymore. I have to take care of my father."

With that, he stormed out of the council chamber. A stray hand reached over and tried to stop him, but Randyll shrugged it off. In a moment he tossed back the tarp that covered the doorway and stepped out onto the muddy road that led back to his home. Back to his father.

They came to this planet light years away to start a new life and escape the dredge of society. Randyll Dougherty was only six when they were chosen as one of the thousand families to board the Nostradamus. They were picked by a lottery, while the wealthy bought their way onto these metallic pilgrim ships. Five years later, they finally reached the home world: Thrae Wen.

"It was supposed to be New Earth, but there was a glitch with the blasted computer," his father explained to him once upon a time. "It read it wrong, and so New Earth became Thrae Wen. For some odd reason, the name stuck."

At the age of sixteen, Randyll figured he'd spent a third of his life on this planet they now called home. But it felt like the old home in many ways. The rich lived in the luxury of machine-cooled comfort in Neo City, a metal monstrosity that loomed over the colony camps like a silent sentinel, with blinking lights for eyes. Those who could not afford to live in the city slept in shanties with canvas roofs overhead, built from the remains of the Nostradamus. It wasn't so different from their home on Earth. Except for the sky.

The sky on Thrae Wen was always a hazy shade of crimson with strange, alien clouds of purple vapor that sometimes blotted out the yellow sun. Those clouds seemed even more foreboding at night when they turned the color of blood and slithered past the pale moons. It took many nights for Randyll to be able to sleep with the shades open. All the while, his father lay dying in the other room.

Back on Earth, his father was a holy man of sorts. He was a believer in a group of faithful who called themselves the Children of Gaia. They denounced technology that possessed any sort of artificial intelligence, which in this day and age, included everything from toaster ovens to wristwatches. His father believed that it was technology that ruined the Earth, and he wasn't alone in that belief.

While his father delivered his sermons and theories to those who would listen, zealots took more extreme measures. There were attacks in the cities, and people were killed. Randyll recalled seeing violent images on the vid-screens of fire and smoke and death. Angry people yelled while mothers held the bloodied and broken bodies of their children. It wasn't long before the Children of Gaia were labeled as terrorists and murderers instead of the peaceful revelations that Randyll's father instilled into his wife and son.

But his father continued to preach to those who would listen, even as the world began to fall apart.

"Keep it simple..." was a personal catechism that his

father would oftentimes repeat to young Randyll. Back on Old Earth, the Dougherty family lived in a modest-sized house without all the modern amenities. When they were cold, his father would chop wood and burn it in the fireplace. When they were hungry, they would eat home-cooked meals prepared painstakingly by his mother. When they got sick, they prayed, and if that didn't work, they would see the doctor—a flesh-and-blood human doctor.

When they were chosen to go, it was very difficult for his father to accept that they would have to leave their home—and even more difficult to climb aboard the Nostradamus, the "contraption of human arrogance and design," as he called it. But his mother begged and pleaded until he finally relented.

Randyll grew up on that ship. He met a few kids his age during his time roaming the silent, metal corridors with the rubber-coated floors. He recalled a close friend by the name of Billy Wilson. The two of them were like "peas in a pod" as his mother would say. They'd go everywhere and do everything together.

Billy had a toy robot that he would sometimes let Randyll play with. Although,Randyll never told his father about the toy. He knew better than to say such a thing to the grouchy, grumbling man who sat in their cozy, high-efficiency apartment and only left to eat in the cafeteria when mother didn't feel like cooking. So he kept it a secret until the accident...

The two boys were playing in the Synth-Park, a recreation of Central Park from New York City. The designers had painstakingly replicated the bushes and the trees and even the bridge that crossed over the lake. That particular morning, the boys sat around ordering the intelligent toy to pick up rocks and stack them one atop one another.

The robot looked like a forest elf with pointed ears and locks of golden hair that spilled down its back. The thing was shorter than either boy, but they treated it like it was another child instead of an automaton. That morning, Randyll noticed something odd about the toy. Stamped on the inside of its left wrist, he saw a bit of metal with a bar-code printed across it.

"What's that?" he asked Billy.

"Oh, it's just his tracking plate," the pudgy boy replied with a shrug. "In case he gets lost or stolen, the authorities can scan his plate and find out who he really belongs to."

"I see," Randyll responded. Just then, the robot elf stopped collecting rocks and slumped over. "Ah, man, it ran out of juice."

"No way. I just charged it last night!" Billy complained, and he walked over to the robot and thumped it with the palm of his hand. "Come on, you stupid hunk of junk!"

Randyll never cared for how Billy treated his things. Several times he'd seen his friend destroy a perfectly good toy just because it wasn't working the way he wanted it to. He saw Billy doing the same to this expensive, high-tech toy, and he almost said something. He almost told him to stop.

"Piece of crap!" Billy growled as he moved to punch the robot. Billy balled his hand into a fist. From his peripheral view, Randyll saw the ocean blue eyes of the elf robot blink and turn toward Billy. It then reached out – lightning fast – and snagged Billy by the forearm.

"Critical error 5 dash 72," the robot said in its digitized voice, then it snapped Billy's arm like a piece of plastic. Randyll heard the sharp sound of the bone breaking. Billy shrieked in agony. He tried to push away the robot but the machine would not release him. Randyll swore he saw the robot smile, and he felt the hackles on his neck rise. He wanted to help his friend, but the sight of the evil machine froze him in his place.

It was the adults that eventually came to the rescue. A man wearing a technician's jumpsuit moved behind the robot and opened a panel on the back of its neck. He pressed a few buttons, and the robot released the boy.

That night, his father gave him a stern lecture when he learned that Randyll was around that "infernal machine". He scolded him and reminded him that they believed in Gaia. That the Earth Mother was polluted and murdered by these machines who were becoming smarter than their creators. He shouted that they were repeating the same old sins by traveling in this giant machine headed to ruin another world.

Randyll was not allowed to see his little friend after the incident.

"Who goes there?" a woman called as Randyll stepped past the tarp that served as a door to the Dougherty domicile.

"It's only me, Trysh," he said, and the near-blind woman nodded at him.

"How's he doing?" he asked, gazing across the room to his father.

"He's been chatty," she said.

"Anything coherent?"

"Oh, bits and pieces but nothing that made much sense to me."

"Well, thanks for watching over him. I can take it from here," Randyll said, approaching his father's bedside.

"Did the council make any decisions?" Trysh asked, reaching for her walking stick.

"No good decisions," Randyll grumbled, and Trysh cackled.

"That's not surprising. Well, if you ever need me, you know where to find me. Good day to you, Michael," Trysh said, motioning toward his father. She found her way out of the Dougherty home and back out into the world.

Randyll took her place on the stool next to his father. Most boys his age were out chasing girls or racing sky skiffs over the sargassi fields. But he was stuck watching his father die because of some alien virus that seemed to only claim the poor. And even more conveniently, it seemed especially fatal to those who called themselves Children of Gaia.

"Don't look so sad, Randy," his dad mumbled as if he could read his son's thoughts."Soon I'll be with your mother and all of our friends and family who returned to Gaia. Free from these shells that we call bodies, we'll become celestial beings of pure light and air and love."

"I know, Dad. I know." Randyll sighed, patting his father on his frail and thin shoulder. His father, Michael, had been a large man with broad shoulders and arms as thick as tree trunks. He was a hard working man, and in many ways, he reminded Randyll of the ancient Earthen story about a railroad worker named John Henry. Old John Henry said he could beat the company's steam-powered hammer that laid down railroad ties, and in the end, he did beat that old contraption, but it cost him his life. Randyll feared that his father's faith and this awful disease would cost him his.

"Shit," Randyll whispered as he saw the blood tears

dribble from his father's eyes. That was how the virus started and that was how it ended. Blood seeped from the eyes like red tears. That's why they called it the Deadly Tears virus.

Randyll took a clean handkerchief and dabbed the cloth in some sterilized water before he applied it to his father's eyes. Slowly, he wiped away the bloody tears while choking back his grief. Randyll felt a lump in the back of his throat and it made him angry. He couldn't show weakness now, not while his father needed him.

"Maybe she'll come, son. Maybe she'll come," Michael Dougherty whispered in his delirium. Oftentimes, he would fall into saying such things. Randyll thought he was talking about Mom.

That night, Randyll tried to sleep while listening to his father's labored breathing. It sounded like someone had stuffed a wet rag down his throat. When the sound stopped, Randyll instantly sat up on his cot and glanced over at his father.

"Dad?" he called, and waited. A second became a minute, a minute became five, and finally he heard his father breathing. It was barely audible, and he breathed a sigh of relief. His father was at least sleeping. He, too, lay back on his flimsy cot and fell into an exhausted slumber.

The next morning, Randyll stood in front of a dirty

mirror over a basin of soapy water, clutching a straightedge razor. He deftly maneuvered the blade with the ivory handle, a relic handed down from his father's father and eventually to him. First, he cut away at the few whiskers, while leaving the tuft of orange hair that clung to his chin. After that, he removed the excess hair from the stripe that ran from his forehead to the back of his skull. His father hated his mohawk.

"Why would you do that to your lovely hair, Randy?" he asked him once.

"All the kids are doing it," he explained, but he knew there was another reason. No one kept their original hair color on Thrae Wen, especially those who lived in the colonies outside of Neo City. Lice were especially prevalent out here and the vibrant colors helped them find and eradicate the little bugs. But, it was also a way that Randyll could fit in with the kids his age, instead of playing the role of his father's caretaker.

When Randyll looked down to rinse his blade, he noticed blood in the basin.

"Dammit," he muttered, feeling around with his wet hand for a knick on his scalp. The worse part about using a straightedge was cutting himself. When he drew back his hand and saw no blood on his fingertips, it baffled him. Randyll glanced at the dirty mirror then and saw a red tear drip from his eye. It trailed down his cheek where it collected along his jaw line before falling into the soapy water.

"No..." he whispered. This couldn't be happening to him. He was only sixteen. He had barely lived a life at all. Another bloody tear fell from his right eye and eventually one welled up in his left. Randyll wanted nothing more than to break down right then, but his father called for him. Summoning up what little strength he still possessed, Randyll grabbed a towel and dabbed at his eyes as he rushed out of the bathroom.

"What is it, Dad?" he asked, trying not to sound annoyed or panicked.

"There are people walking around out there. So many people," he muttered, and Randyll sighed. He didn't have time to cater to his father's hallucinations; he had problems of his own to deal with. But not for much longer, he thought.

"Dad, there's nobody out—" he started to say, until he pulled back the tattered curtain. To his disbelief, he saw a crowd of colonists lined along the muddy road that cut a swath through the shacks and shanties. He saw familiar faces – neighbors and fellow shipmates– staring off into the distance.

"What are they doing out there?" his father demanded, attempting to sit up. Randyll reached over and gently guided him back to his pillow.

"I'll go outside and find out. Just be patient," he whispered, still clutching the bloodied towel. He gingerly dabbed at his eyes and walked through the bit of tarp that served as a door. Once outside, the cacophony of people whispering echoed through the neighborhood. He spotted the old blind woman, Trysh, standing nearby.

"What's going on?" he asked as she leaned on her walking stick. She glared up at him with milky eyes. Her wispy hair fluttered as a light breeze wafted through the colony.

"I'm not sure. I think it's the Samaritans bringing us food," she croaked, and then gestured toward the end of the road. Coming up the hill, Randyll spotted two cloaked figures wearing black and white, and trailing behind them was a young woman. He could not quite make her out behind the Sacred Sisters and their wide-brimmed hats, so he stood gawking like the rest of the colonists.

"It's her!" one person muttered, and the crowd seemed to surge toward the Sisters and the strange young woman hiding behind their flowing robes.

He watched as the Sisters placed one foot in front of the other, carrying baskets of what he assumed were provisions. He caught a glimpse of the woman behind them. She seemed tall, and for a split second, he thought he saw shimmering locks of pink-dyed hair.

He felt a bloody tear escape and dribble down his cheek. Randyll quickly dabbed at it and stared at the crimson stains on the already discolored towel. It scared him to see his own blood. It terrified him to think that with every drop, he was that much closer to death. He was so caught up with his own mortality that he never noticed how the crowd parted before him, nor did he see the Sacred Sisters looming over him. Randyll just stared at that towel until the girl with pink hair spoke.

"I've come to help," she said in a sweet and innocent voice. He immediately looked up and gasped as he stared into the crystalline pools of her vibrant eyes. She was beautiful; that much he could tell. He thought she was close to his age, maybe a few years younger, but she was very tall. Taller than Randyll by a few inches.

"I...I..." he muttered, trying to find the words.

"Shh," she said, pursing her delicate lips as she placed her index finger in front of her mouth. "Just hold still and it will all be over."

Randyll swallowed as the girl raised her other hand. She lifted her slender fingers, fanning them out until her palm rested mere inches from his forehead. However, she did not touch him. Randyll felt another bloody tear begin to slide down his cheek. He wanted desperately to wipe it away with the soiled towel, more out of embarrassment than anything else.

"It's all right. You'll be all right," the girl said, and

to his disbelief, a pulse of light passed out of her hand and blinded him momentarily. Randyll felt a numbing warmth overtake his body. He stumbled backwards but steady hands reached out to prevent him from falling.

When he could see again, he stared at the reddish haze of the sky above. He blinked several times before settling his gaze on the Sacred Sisters who held him by the arms. They smiled at him with kind, ageless faces, staring at him with deep, brown eyes, unblinking but full of reverent concern.

And then he saw the girl with pink hair walking away. Frantically, Randyll pushed himself past the Sisters and called out for the girl.

"Wait! Please, you have to help my father! Please!" he begged, instinctively reaching for the girl. However, the Sacred Sisters stopped him in his tracks. He was surprised by their strength. Fortunately, the girl turned to him, and with a brief nod, she allowed Randyll to lead her to the shack he called home.

Randyll held the tarp for the girl as she approached the doorway. The Sacred Sisters tried to block her way, but she gave them a disapproving glance, shaking her lovely head sternly. The nuns seemed to understand and allowed her to enter the shanty while they stood guard outside.

As she crossed the threshold, the girl with pink hair glanced around the shack. She paused before a rickety table with a collection of photographs nestled safely in glass frames. Randyll watched her, almost impatiently, as he stood next to his father. Michael Dougherty studied the girl, bloody tears welling up in his yellowed eyes.

"Please. Please, help him," Randyll reiterated. She nodded and swiftly crossed over to his father's bedside.

"Who is she?" his father asked, before he broke into another coughing fit.

"I'm here to help," she whispered, kneeling before the dying man. Randyll watched as she raised her hand over his father. Randyll was just about to warn him to close his eyes when he saw the flash of light for the second time. He heard his father gasp as he turned away, squinting against the brilliant light.

Randyll did not open his eyes until he heard his father cry out. Finally, he blinked away the firework display that played across his vision and looked at his father. He did not see the bloody tears forming at the corner of his eyelids. For once, his father did not seem as if he were standing with one foot already in the grave. It was a miracle, and it was the second one he had experienced today.

Randyll heard a rustling from the doorway just then, and when he turned, he saw the girl leaving the shanty. Immediately, he rushed after her. He couldn't let her go without thanking her for what she'd done. This time he did touch her.

He encircled her slender wrist with his shaking fingers, and she turned toward him with a smile.

"He will be fine now, as will you," she said.

Randyll was wrong when he thought she was just beautiful. When he looked upon the smooth and flawless skin of this girl, he knew she was radiant. Angelic might have been a better word. However, it was then that he felt something strange on her wrist. Without thinking, he glanced down and turned his hand so that the underside of her wrist pointed toward the ceiling.

Embedded in the skin, he found a slender piece of metal, and imprinted on the metal was a bar-code. But Randyll knew that it was called a tracking plate.

"Is there anything else that you require?" the girl asked, gently removing her wrist from his grip. He blinked, feeling momentarily dumbfounded, until he thought of a question.

"What is your name?" he asked, again looking into her crystalline eyes.

"Elysia," she said. "What's yours?"

"Randyll. But you can call me Randy."

"It was nice to meet you, Randy," she politely replied with a single nod. Afterwards, she exited into the throng of people waiting to receive her healing touch. She left Randyll standing in the doorway, unsure if any of this was real or not.

"Randy? What are you doing over there?" his father asked, sounding stronger now. Randyll shook his head, trying to drive away the questions that already bombarded his brain. He smiled at his dad and sauntered over to his bedside.

"You never told me...who was that girl?" he asked, looking up at his son with healthy eyes. For a moment, the very briefest of moments, Randyll considered telling his father the truth.

"She called herself Elysia," he replied instead.

"Elysia?" his father said. "What a pretty name."

"Yes," Randyll agreed, taking his father's hand. He then kneeled on the floor, silently thanking Gaia for saving the two of them. "It is a pretty name."

About the Author

Josh Schwartzkopf lives in Belleville, IL with his wife and son. His first short story, *Vortex,* was featured in a military-themed science fiction anthology called Battlespace, and proceeds from sales of the anthology went to the Warrior Cry Project to help wounded veterans purchase musical instruments. He has written many other short stories, which have been published in Kzine, Postcard Shorts, and SpeckLit, among others. When he's not writing, Josh enjoys spending time with his family and reading anything he can get his hands on.

Property
Cathleen Townsend

"Mr. Morgan, you are the property of the Republic of California." I swung my gavel down.

The man looked stunned—as well he might. The chances of him ever working off his debt bondage were slim at best. I exited the courthouse and was confronted with yet another distraught wife on the steps.

"Judge Vickers, please, it wasn't his fault. We'll pay it all back."

My eyes flicked toward her. I had a limited number of pardons available. Some of them even went to people with payment plans. Since California guaranteed all debts, judges were encouraged to get as much back as we could.

"How?" Best to keep it short.

"I can take another job. We can sell our car and take transit. We'll figure something out—"

I shook my head; castles in the air wouldn't suffice,

and it was best not to give her false hope. "I'm afraid your husband will be sold to pay his creditors." It wasn't as though the work camps were inhumane.

"But what about our children? What am I supposed to do?" She actually put her hand on my arm.

I'd had enough; I shrugged her hand off. "Ms. Morgan, because of people like your husband, the Republic of California cannot afford to help you." Everyone knew the old United States had collapsed over indebtedness. We'd learned our lessons, or at least some of us had. "I don't know what you'll do, but I strongly advise against going into debt." I shook my head as I walked away. Days like this made me wonder why I'd wanted to be a judge in the first place.

The answer to that question was waiting in the parking structure, in the person of my colleague, Judge Warner. "And how was your day, Arthur?" His expression was smug. He must have found the day financially rewarding.

I sighed. "Nothing worth your time." Warner was involved in property management. I'd passed him a juicy tidbit a couple months ago, but today had been nothing but cases without assets. "How about you?"

"I have something that might interest you. The defendant is offering commercial insurance policies as payment. The discount rate looks to be enough to make it worth your while, but I lack the expertise to be certain."

We had to be careful; too many blank pardons and our numbers would be off. Voters wanted to see us saving California tax dollars, not building our retirement plans. Discretion was required.

Fortunately, this was right up my alley; I held my hand out for the folder. "We'll go ahead and transfer the case to my court." I unlocked my car, settled into my leather seat, and thumbed through it. It looked promising. Although now Warner and I would be square, and I preferred it when people owed me favors. Still, markers were worthless if you never called them in.

Late that evening, I smiled as I finished my detailed summary of assets. California could definitely grant clemency in this case. Insurance was so elegant—you received all the money up front. It certainly wasn't the fault of the business that this fellow had ended up in debtor's court. Fortunately for him, he had something to buy his way back out again.

The next day, I passed the paperwork to Harry, my partner who ran the payday loan side of our business.

He gave it several minutes' scrutiny. "I don't see any problems. I suppose you want me to handle transferring ownership?"

It wouldn't do to have a judge openly taking over debtor assets; we all had partners to handle that. It had certainly catapulted mine to wealth much faster than he would have otherwise achieved. Harry enjoyed his flashy sports cars and trips abroad, but I had to admit, he held up his end with good management.

Harry cleared his throat. "I should have the quarterly reports for the loan business by the end of the month. I think you'll be pleased." Sudden amusement came and went on his face. "Or not." Harry and I had an ongoing rivalry as to who could generate better figures. The current forfeit was a week in Hawaii. I wasn't worried, though; he hadn't seen mine. A week on the beach was just what I needed.

I returned to my routine for a time, seeing cases and passing the occasional favor. I comforted myself that in another year I could retire and never be further than ten feet from a beach or a bikini-clad beauty. I had a stack of real estate opportunities in tropical locales that I kept on my nightstand for reading before bed. Belize was supposed to have fantastic scuba-diving.

I awoke to a low grinding rumble with a soprano accompaniment of rattling glassware. I knocked the brochures aside, fumbling for the remote. The quake didn't last long, and I fervently hoped it was an anomaly, with an epicenter here in Sacramento. The financial damage from a quake like this wouldn't be much more than a hiccup. Another year of working, tops.

But the news coverage showed the Bay Bridge, unusable with a new one-foot drop, and the airport in San Francisco with runways scarred by gaping fissures. Fires and looting would complete the destruction of property. My profanity didn't drown out the newscaster's words. "Preliminary seismic reports are calling this at least an 8.1, possibly higher, with the epicenter at or near San Francisco."

I ran a hand through my hair and paced. The recent accounts we'd taken on weren't our only exposure in this area, and earthquake policies had figured heavily into the mix. I hoped Harry's figures were damn good, or we'd have to sell off rental properties to help cover this. We could put it back together, but shit! We were looking at ten years down the drain.

I worked up a set of summaries and sent off a missive to Harry, giving him a heads up. I spent the rest of the day in court, listening half-heartedly to cases, none of which had assets that could bail us out.

That evening, unable to wait on his reply, I swung by Harry's office. He got down to business right away, pushing his own set of neat figures across the desk.

I barely stopped myself from crumpling the paper. "It doesn't look like either of us will be going to Hawaii anytime soon."

Harry shrugged. "It could be much worse. We've been careful. The apartment buildings will all have to go, but we can cover the debts. Both the loans and insurance bring in steady income. And your pardons will recoup the asset loss."

Easy for him to say. He was in his thirties, not his forties.

I put a smile on my face. "I suppose it can't be helped. Let's do the paperwork and get the real estate on the market. I don't want to be pressured to sell and have to take less than they're worth." I spent a couple hours signing away any possibility of near-future retirement and took a deep breath as I walked to my car. Better to have it done than hanging over me. While Harry liquidated real estate, I would simply shift my focus to rebuilding.

I went back to work and watched case after case go through with no possibility of profit. It was always a matter of feast or famine, but the timing was unfortunate in the extreme. I scanned the documents of the wretches in front of me, but even if I lowered my standards, there was nothing here worth my time.

When I finally received Harry's report, all the blood ran from my face, and I collapsed in my leather chair. He'd definitely consolidated assets; I had to give him that. He'd taken the papers I'd signed and liquidated everything, but then he'd dissolved the partnership and fled California. He was probably somewhere on a beach in South America. I had nothing.

The next few months were a haze of misery, trying to work deals. I appealed to my colleagues, one by one, offering what few possessions I still had; cars, art, my home in the exclusive neighborhood by the river. I'd allowed myself to hope, but I knew my answer when their eyes slid away. There were juicier opportunities to be had. My few remaining possessions weren't worth using up a pardon. The few times I tried to invoke any kind of solidarity, they walked away. How could this be happening? I had been so careful.

I spent the short time that remained to me in my home. California would sell everything after I left. I drank my collection of fine wine, and on the final day, I packed all I could into the single bag I'd be allowed to keep. I'd had custom locks installed on it; there would be many men at the work camps who would be looking to even the score. I shook my head when it was done. I'd taken more when I went to Paris.

I made the final trip to the courthouse. I attempted to meet Warner's eyes, desperately hoping for clemency, but his eyes were on the papers in front of him.

The gavel came down. "Mr. Vickers, you are now the property of the Republic of California."

About the Author

Cathleen Townsend was born and raised in California. Her greatest passions are history, speculative fiction, and the incredible beauty of her home state. She enjoys hiking and horseback-riding, and she's always entranced by a good story, whatever the genre or medium.

She and her husband have reside in the Sierra Nevada foothills, with an Arab horse who thinks mud is a fashion statement, a German Shepherd who takes her security responsibilities seriously, an angelic border collie, and a cat who is certain he can whoop the shepherd anytime he likes.

Her stories have been publish in Every Day Fiction and Thinkerbeat. Dragon Hoard and Other Tales will be released in December of 2015.

To contact her or find out more about Cathleen's work, visit her website: cathleentownsend.com. She tweets @ CathleenTowns.

GOD Is in the Rain
Nemma Wollenfang

When Kay was five, she would sit in the window of Gran's New York apartment and watch as rain lashed the sky. *Nature's tears*. The drops cut clear paths through the dirt and grime, cleaning the glass in a way that frail Gran could not. The world had been a very different place back then; some would say it was hostile, some would say it was free. As a child, Kay did not have an opinion either way; the world just was, and the rain just fell.

Gran used to say that God was in the rain. Twenty years on, that idea became reality.

"Another Stepford drone," Earl muttered darkly as he eyed the man entering the diner.

"A G.O.D. infectee?" Kay asked, cocking her head. "How can you tell?"

"It's that smarmy little smile," he grimaced with obvious distaste as he flipped his burgers, "the way he looks so blissfully *happy*. No one ever looks that happy—not even happy people look that happy. Then there's the suit, the air-brushed face, the sleek-neat hair. Bet not a one of them is outta place. And look at the way he just…floats."

"Floats." Kay raised an eyebrow. People did not *float*.

"You know what I mean." He tossed another hammy. Below it, the grill sizzled and spat fat. He frowned. "You serve him. I can't stand his like."

"Hello," she said as she approached the table. Pad open, pen out – low tech. "Welcome to Earl's Diner. I'm Kakiya Moran, your waitress for today. Can I start you with a drink?"

The man had a handsome mien, but all infectees wore a far-off expression when addressed that made people uneasy. Kay tried not to notice.

"Gracious server," The man inclined his head, "I will begin with a water, if you would be so kind, followed by a *Lettuca* salad, no dressing."

Lettuca salad: the plain food of the plain-minded. All G.O.D. infectees were vegan, but few would imbibe any of the more delectable fruits and vegetables – just *Lettuca*, ice-lettuce. Specially formulated dietary supplements made up for the rest of their bodily needs. Maximum nutritional intake—minimal taste. They believed that anything more was gluttonous.

"Gotcha." Kay wrote the order and moved away. Best not to linger.

"Straight leaves, Earl," she called, clipping the order up, "hold the decoupage."

"Pah," he said. A salad was already waiting. Infectees were nothing if not predictable.

The Government had released the first batch of G.O.D.'s – Guidance and Obedience Devices – into a reservoir that fed a small town in Illinois with a bad rep. The micro-nanites, when consumed, were designed to target the primitive hypothalamic areas of the brain that induced fierce and violent impulses, and once those areas activated, to neutralize them.

The first trials led to an unprecedented success. Crime rates dropped, divorce became a thing of the past, and even littering ceased. Good behavior and fine manners abounded.

It was perfect. Too perfect.

People became shadows of their former selves, lifeless drones who only ate and slept and functioned in the most basic sense. In other words, "model citizens".

The Government was thrilled. They called the invention "the key to world peace." They demanded more. But even had they not, the G.O.D. nanites would have spread. The summer of '42 was the hottest on record—global warming at its peak—and in the heat the reservoir had dried out. The water had evaporated into the atmosphere and taken the G.O.D.'s along with it. And the nanites had a replication mandate built into their programming. After that, there was no stopping the spread. They became airborne; they evolved into roaming hives. Now they were everywhere – policing the world in their own automated way. Keeping the peace.

As Kay delivered the salad, her sister entered the diner. Maia was another Government success, a "model citizen", and it stung every time Kay saw her.

"Hey, can I get a refill over here?" a customer hollered – a regular citizen, clearly.

"Maia," Kay sighed, feeling the weight of her eight-hour shift, "can you, please?"

"Of course, sweet sister," she smiled, her blue eyes empty. "Anything to ease the flow of your life." Taking Kay's apron, she set to working the next shift.

Once they had been so much alike: vibrant, snarky, quick-tempered. Now they were polar opposites. It had happened a month ago, at their home in Aurora. Maia had fought with her husband over something trivial. She'd slapped Mike. To be fair, he'd hit her first. That did not stop the G.O.D.'s from targeting her, too, as they swarmed the house. Maia must have heard them coming, Kay had from across the street. She'd run for them, for her sister. But Roth had tackled her into the lawn. Sweet, caring, *stupid* Roth. He'd held her down as metallic mist obscured the sky. There had been no screams, only telling silence.

Maia and Mike settled their differences that night. They have not fought since. But Maia was not the same girl, never would be again. If only it had not rained…

"Kakiya," Maia said now, standing before her with a coffeepot. Kay jumped. Maybe the drones *did* float. "I meant to tell you as I arrived. Roth is outside."

Through the diner's glass walls, Kay could see him, propped against his motorbike by the 7-Eleven across the way. He had on his black leathers, worn jeans and boots – standard Roth. Jet hair hung about his face, negligently cut, and his skin was tanned. But even at a distance, the shadows under his eyes were stark.

He looked weary. And Kay knew why.

"I don't want to talk to him."

"You should. It's been a month," Maia hummed, in that eerily detached way infectees did. "Perhaps with gentle understanding you will settle your differences and come to know the peace that Mike and I share. You were such a solid couple once."

Kay gritted her teeth. Maia didn't know any better. Words had been said that could never be taken back. "Thanks for delivering the message."

She nodded and moved along, easily absorbed in her server duties, while Kay took the back exit. Not ten feet past the stinking garbage and Roth was at the alley's mouth.

The man was a bloodhound.

"We need to talk," he said, tossing down his Marlboro, then stubbing it out with a boot.

"Not now," she hissed as she pushed past. *Not ever.*

"Kay," he grated, following on her heels, "there was nothing we could do. They'd have taken us, too, you know that, especially after we'd de-magged our systems. I had to—"

"I don't want to hear it."

Always he had to rationalize—always he had to explain. Why could he not just act?

"Kay, please." Roth snatched her elbow, hauling her to a halt. The action made her skid and nearly fall, her sneakers caught on a slick patch of pavement. But his grip steadied her. And she glared at him for it. His strength had prevented her from saving her sister too.

"Miss," an airy voice said, "is everything all right?"

It was the *Lettuca*-salad man. He blinked at them benignly from the diner's entrance.

Only then did Kay realize what this looked like, how hard Roth gripped her, how much she glared. Hostility practically crackled between them—exactly what G.O.D.'s adhered to.

"Everything is fine," Roth said, releasing his hold and withdrawing.

"Yes, fine," Kay smiled pleasantly, "thank you for your concern, kind citizen."

She added the last to appease the drone. They loved nothing if not their formalities.

The infectee returned inside.

"Be more careful, Roth," she hissed, rounding on him. "Or we'll both be screwed. Any excuse and those things call in the troops." The *troops* being a silvery swarm of their misty brethren. With a huff, she searched her pockets. "Damn, I forgot my keys."

In her haste to avoid Roth, she'd left them in Earl's office. Ignoring Roth, she shoved through the diner's door and paused. Everyone was very still, even Maia.

"Everybody quiet," a man grated, clearly agitated as he waved something around.

Sleek and black – a gun.

Most sat frozen. Some held their hands up. A mother

whimpered, clutching her boy close. A server set down her trembling coffeepot. Kay's throat grew dry.

"This is a robbery, so just stay calm!" the man yelled, a hand fisting his hair. "CALM!"

No one acted otherwise. He alone appeared not to be. The blood-shot eyes, semi-shaved buzz-cut, and bulging vein at his temple only added to his derangement.

Backing up to keep them all in sight, he tossed a bag over the counter to Earl.

"Money, in the bag," he hissed, "all of it, now!"

Earl complied, his eyes careful. Kay had not moved from her spot by the door. Now she realized that the robber would likely have to go past her. Should she move? Was that wise?

Thoughts ground to a halt as Maia meekly approached the man, her face blank.

"Kind sir, there is no need for violence. If you would but sit, I could fetch a beverage t—"

"Shut up, drone!" The gun pointed at Maia.

She didn't think. Kay never did. Quick on the draw, her father used to say, never one to fight instinct. She didn't now as instinct led her to snatch his wrist, and twist it up. The gun blasted once as Kay landed a fist on his nose. She put all of her strength into that shot.

Teeth cut skin, tiny nasal bones crunched.

The man hit the counter head-first, then the stool, then the floor.

Out cold.

The diner stood frozen as if in an adrenaline-fuelled dream. Hushed, as all gazes fell on her. Not grateful, but pitying. Why?

The door slammed open and its little bell tinkled as Roth charged in.

"What…" He gasped, taking in the scene. "Oh, Kay, no…"

The gun fell from her limp fingers to clatter on the linoleum. It echoed loudly. At her feet, the man lay unmoving, while the drones regarded him with expressionless eyes. His mind was practically forfeit. She'd seen it before. Once the G.O.D.'s swarmed, they would seize his body, invading until his eyes grew dim. The light within, the spark that ignited all living beings, would flicker… and extinguish. To be replaced with a soulless stare.

But he was not the only one to partake in this violent act.

Realization: The pitying gazes suddenly made sense.

"Oh," Kay gasped. "I'll be neutralized too!"

There was no way out. G.O.D.'s did not discriminate between right and wrong; the undeserving and the deserving. They just did their job with cold, detached efficiency.

Horror filled her as she met Earl's gaze. He mouthed something she could not hear. Her ears were ringing. No, that was the G.O.D.'s. The hum was starting, like the buzz of a far-off hive. Steel mist would soon arise; a metallic eclipse of silver bees that would descend on the diner, and her.

Roth snatched her hand, she thought for comfort, but before anyone could move they were out the door and dashing down the street.

"W-what are you doing?" Kay gasped, trying to keep up as she stumbled at his side.

"No matter what you might think of me, Kakiya, I'm not about to stand by and let you become a fucking zombie."

"Is there another option?"

His only response was to toss her his helmet as he kick-started the bike and told her to get on. The feel of his jacket in her hands, the way her legs wound so perfectly around his thighs, was at once familiar and unwelcome. Right now she was not about to complain. The engine roared as they tore off down the street, it barely obscured the rising hum.

There's nowhere you can hide, so they say, once the G.O.D.'s start to track. They always find their marks. Legions of runners had failed before; so it was unlikely that Kay would fair differently. She knew this. So why did she let Roth try? Because she was afraid that's why. No one wants to forfeit their mind.

Six hours and two brief rest-stops later found them on the outskirts of some nameless highway, shivering in the parking lot of a Motel 6. One room, Roth booked. One bed.

"Make yourself at home," he said.

Kay had no clothes, only her uniform – a horridly short, turquoise thing with pink borders. Earl's fashion sense left something to be desired. There was a bathrobe. She changed into that, yearning for a hot shower. The idea of what the water contained stopped her.

Roth must have thought ahead. He silently handed her a bottle of Spring Water as she reappeared. "Magnetised," he said at her questioning look. "G.O.D.-free."

That was all well and good for now. But what about later? How long could they last?

"Have you ever heard of anyone outrunning those things?" Kay asked as she settled on the bed. Roth stood sentinel at the window, drapes tugged shut. "I thought it was impossible."

"It's not *impossible*," he said, peeking out, "it's improbable."

"And that's better?"

No response. Kay picked at her robe.

"I'm just surprised you didn't leave me there, like you did with Maia." *Low blow.*

The curtain swung as he dropped it. "I didn't just *leave* Maia—you know that."

Those steely eyes bored into hers; neither blue nor truly grey. *Like the sky before a storm.* Little had changed in their month apart. He was still strikingly beautiful; still desirable. He read her appraisal easily.

"There was a time when you said I was devastatingly devilish." He grinned.

"There was a time when I said I loved you."

The grin vanished. "You could be more appreciative. I did just save your ass."

True. Why was she baiting him? But then, she'd always been that way. Sometimes Kay wondered why he put up with her grit. She was reckless, she was rash—a prime candidate for G.O.D. neutralization. It was astonishing she hadn't been targeted years ago. Him, too.

"That'll need tending to." Roth gestured to her hand where the robber's teeth had sliced – ugly, congealed, burgundy. "Wounds like that go bad fast. Here."

She sat still as he pulled out a first-aid kit and cleaned and bandaged. His hands were rough and calloused but gentle; a mechanic's hands.

Why *had* Roth stuck around this long? Kay guessed that in a world where gentility and civility were not just paramount, but enforced, other qualities were rare in people. Perhaps that was what drew him, the spark of the primitive in her. Something passionate, something natural, something *human*. "Flammable, yet fragile," he'd once commented of her, not long after they'd made love. The memory made Kay's cheeks flush. Her eyes dropped.

There was a dark stain on the carpet—sticky, likely cola.

"Do you really think I have a chance?" she asked the floor as he finished up.

"Wouldn't be here if I didn't."

"That doesn't really answer my question." Kay pulled back her hand.

Deep sigh. "Here in Cincinnati I met someone a way back. He told me stuff, taught me how to magnetize water and de-mag our blood to clear it of inert nanites, like I did for us."

Kay recalled it well, the day he had brought home a glowing blue device. He'd said then that it was a way for them to remain free. He'd meant to use it on Maia and Mike too.

"Highly illegal in the US, o'course," he chuckled, "but worth it if it saves us. That's what destroyed the few G.O.D.'s already in your system and stopped them activating the second you clocked that guy. It won't work on large-scale infections but it does for the small stuff. It's temporary, though, shelf-life of about a month. That's why I was at the diner today. I wanted to renew your dose. But there were other things he told me…"

Kay blinked, absorbing all that. "What things?"

He stashed the box and returned to his post by the window. Neon lights filtered through the gap; illuminating his shadowy frame.

"Some people don't like the way things have gone. They don't like the way our world has turned." He paused, flicking the drape. "Some people plan to do something about it."

Kay frowned. "What people?"

"Get some sleep, Kakiya. I'll keep watch."

He would say nothing more, no matter how much

Kay pestered.

*

Windows rattled, the door burst off its hinges. No light shone through, no sun could breach the metallic wall. The buzz drowned all sound. It pierced, it *screeched*, like nails being driven into her brain. Kay clamped hands over her ears and pressed into the headboard.

Her mind twisted in strange ways, recalling more clearly the details from the diner. She knew now what Earl had been mouthing: *Run.*

She awoke with a start, gasping, sweating, trapped by the sheets. She fought them off.

Roth was nowhere in sight. The room was deserted. Had he left? Washed his hands of her? No, Roth would never do that. Had they found him then? Had Kay lost him too?

There was a faint patter – the telltale strikes of drops on the roof.

The door opened and shut.

"Rain's started," Roth huffed as he shook out his hair, slouching out of his jacket. "As long as you keep away from the windows, the G.O.D.'s won't be able to scan for you. You're safe in here. Shelter, one of mankind's first and greatest inventions—"

Kay was out of bed and in his arms before he could finish.

"What?" he breathed, eyes surprised and searching.

"You were gone when I woke up. I-I thought…" There was no need to finish. Roth knew, she could tell, just by the way she quivered.

They were broken as a pair. They were a ragged wound that may never heal. But despite their estrangement, losing Roth was something that Kay could not fathom.

The kiss came hard and fast, surprising them both. But he did not pull away. The taste of him was glaringly familiar, the zest of lemon, chased by the bite of whiskey. He'd been drinking. She walked backwards, leading them to the bed.

He didn't argue. He didn't even try.

Later, as they lay wrapped around each other, hair hectic in ruffled sheets, Kay's fears started to resurface. It was easy to forget in the afterglow, a haven flooded with endorphins.

"Does this mean you forgive me?" Roth asked, in that sultry way of his; all male satisfaction as he stretched underneath her.

Kay trailed her fingers along the planes of his chest while Roth twirled a honey-lock around his fingers. She'd highlighted it this summer; he seemed to approve.

"It means I had no right to be mad at you in the first place." The words were carefully measured. "I was grieving for my sister. I lashed out. But you didn't deserve it."

It was as good an apology as Kay would ever give. Roth said nothing, just reclined on his back and stared at the cracked paint on the old ceiling. Kay recognized the reprieve.

"Why were you outside?"

"Supplies," he said, nodding to the shopping bags by the door. Kay had barely noticed them before. "Magnetised water, energy bars, beef jerky, oil. All the best a gas station has to offer. Found a gun, too; we'll need it where we're going. Plus I met an old contact, the one I told you of." He held her gaze significantly. "Have you heard of the anti-G.O.D. movement?"

The AGM. She nodded slowly. There had been hints on the news, whispers and hushed gossip.

"From what I've heard," he continued, "a rebel cell in the south has developed some kind of weapon, a way to counteract the nanites."

"That sounds too good to be true. How would it work, anyway?"

"Some kind of EMP-repulsion tech." With a sigh, he ran fingers through his disheveled bed-head. It flopped back into his face. "If we can find 'em…"

Kay's fingers stopped their roaming. "Seems like a bit of a long-shot, doesn't it?"

Roth grinned, in that charmingly crooked way Kay was so used to. "Always the pessimist." He clucked her chin.

"Where would we start?"

Sand swept up from the tarmac in copper vortexes as the bike hurtled down the I-30. It was one of the few roads still capable of running low-tech transport; all others had been updated to support hover-cars and neo-trikes, and Roth had to deftly skirt the mounting craters that pockmarked its length. Kay was in it for the long haul, letting Roth lead the way. They were headed for the Mexican border. The theory: It didn't rain as much there. G.O.D.'s were fragile machines, and they needed humidity to function: rain, fog, vapor. That's why crime was rampant in the south. Phoenix was the new Chicago. Drier, hotter climates were the key to survival now. At least for Kay.

They pulled up at another motel in Arkansas, in a place called Hope.

Roth said it was a good omen.

"Not too long until we reach Dallas," he grinned. "From there, it's on to San Antonio, and then Monterrey. That's where our people will be."

Our people. He spoke as if they were already two among their number.

"Should take a few days but you've never minded road-tripping." He grinned.

Roth smiled a lot that day, the way he had when they were young and naïve and stupid, when they were new to travel and had no cares, when they had busked on roadsides, and he'd gifted her with a nickname. The usual hardness in his eyes was absent.

His head was filled with plans for their future.

Did they really have one? With the current situation, it didn't seem likely, even with his talk of repulsion-tech and freedom and grand AGM-revolutionaries. He was living in a bubble. One Kay was afraid to pop.

So instead of facing harsh reality, she lived in it along with him. Enjoying each moment as it came.

They rode the highways from dawn until dusk. They made love in motels and drank cheap beer from aluminum cans. They watched old-style cable and wished away the rain.

Kay never thought too long on anything. Though sometimes her mind drifted... Could they live with themselves being *that way*? As yet another Maia and Mike? The world was now filled with ranks of those. Couples that Roth despised.

While he prepared a bath for them of kettle-heated, magnetized H^2O, Kay thought on it. The daredevil would be gone. His smile would no longer be crooked or mischievous. The Roth that remained would not be Roth. It would be a vacant mimic, a drone. *A slate wiped clean.* The notion brought needles to her eyes.

And as they tangled in the tub, caught in the throes, not all the water that decorated her cheeks was magnetized.

They may have been a broken wound, in the process of uncertain healing, but he would still fight like a bear to protect her. Was she exploiting this stalwart quality to save her own skin? She often wondered as they travelled. After all, the G.O.D.'s were tracking her, not him.

Eventually, she told him as much and suggested he leave. The outskirts of Laredo were as good as anywhere for him to start a new life. He scoffed and waved away her concerns.

"What point would there be to a life without you?"

Kay woke early and carefully extricated herself from their bed. Roth mumbled something incomprehensible and rolled over, deep in sleep. One last look, she promised herself; A last goodbye. There was no other way; if he were awake, he would stop her.

Gathering her things, she tip-toed to the sliding door of their motel suite and touched the drapes. The air was chill. Her skin prickled at the temperature drop, and Kay pulled her collar up. Frost? But it was nowhere near winter…

The curtains opened onto a drenched desert-scape, all color darkened to rusty red. It had rained during the night. Moisture had collected on the glass before her nose.

There was a bright flash. The scan was swift and im-personal, and finite.

"Kay!"

The thud of feet, a rush, and Roth snatched her arm. His grip was tight, like a boa's, cutting the blood flow and leaving welts as he backed them away.

Mercurial droplets fused on the glass, humming as they danced like miniature ballerinas. The sound grew and grew.

"You can leave, you know," she said, her voice oddly vacant.

"What?"

"I never should have let you risk yourself as much as

you have for me. But I wanted more time. Leave now. You haven't committed any violence. They won't target you. If you—"

With a strangled grimace, he aimed a gun high at the roiling fog. -

And emptied all six rounds.

Glass shattered. No impact. The fluid mercury swallowed them whole.

Kay sighed, her eyes flitting shut. *Always the martyr.* He'd damned himself too. And to think that at one time she'd wished he'd "just act".

"It was never going to work," she said, "was it?"

The G.O.D.'s tracked their prey well; none had ever escaped, none ever would. The storm of titanium rose up from the crystal fragments to obscure the pale dawn light; a uniform hive of scraping metal.

Their bubble had officially popped.

"Eyes on me," he said.

The hum elevated to a screeching roar. And Roth wrapped her in his arms.

His will alone was not shelter enough.

That winter they bought an apartment in New York that overlooked Central Park. Minimalist; white paint, wood floors, clear open windows. Anything more would have been excess. Roth had said it was time for a new start after Earl had asked Kay, most abruptly, to leave his diner. He did not wish her to work for him any longer. In fact, he had seemed very distressed when they had returned and greeted him cordially. Tears had filled his eyes.

"One o' you is hard enough to stomach, but two? No, I can't…"

Kay could not understand his upset, but then, he was not as enlightened as they. He did not understand the peace that came with the G.O.D.s' presence. Perhaps one day he would.

As Kay sat on the window-sill, Roth leaned over and kissed her head. No smile.

"When I was little, my grandmother had a place like this," she said conversationally, "I used to sit by her window and watch the rain fall." Kay traced a droplet, following its lonely path with a single finger. *Nature's tears.* They washed off the pane. She cocked her head placidly and looked up to the water-filled sky. Slate-grey clouds rumbled as she told Roth, "She used to say that God is in the rain."

And if you looked close, at each individual bead, there was the tiniest swirl of silver.

About the Author

Nemma Wollenfang is an MSC Postgraduate in Vector Biology and Parasitology, who studied at Keele, Salford and Manchester Universities. In the latter part of her studies, she researched ticks and Lyme disease in the Cumbrian Lake District, but now she volunteers at a local animal rescue. In her free time, she has flown falcons, participated in archeological excavation digs and, of course, read great books. Her focus now is writing, both science-fiction and historical, preferably with a romantic thread to spice up the storyline. In 2014, she won first place in the Steampunk Style Short Story Competition run by Steampunk Journal, with her entry, Clockwork Evangeline, which was published by *Titan Books* online. Her work has been short-listed on several occasions and has appeared or is upcoming in a number of publications, including: *Come Into the House* (Corazon Books), *Gothic Science Fiction Short Stories* (Flame Tree Publishing), and *Calliope Magazine*. Her unpublished novel was also short-listed for an international novel award in 2014, and twice more in 2015 (she is currently editing). Follow her on twitter: @NemmaW. Publishers Endnotes

Publishers End Notes

We hope you enjoyed A Bleak New World. If you did, we'd ask you to share it. In today's book world, small presses like ours rely on fans like you sharing the love of our stories. You can do this by telling your friends and family, and posting reviews to websites like Amazon and Goodreads.

We couldn't continue without your support and to say thank you we want to give you a free book. Just sign up for our email list and we will send you a digital copy of another great title from Raven International Publishing.

Sign up at www.RavenInternationalPublishing.com

Thanks so much, we can't do this without you!